Touch My Brother and You Die

내 동생 건들면 너희는 다 죽은 목숨이다

WRITTEN BY MORPHO

EDITIO

PUBLISHING

Touch My Brother and You Die

© Morpho

Cover Illustration by MUMONG

This is a work of fiction. Names, characters, businesses, places, events, locales, and incidents are either the products of the author's imagination or used in a fictitious manner. Any resemblance to actual persons, living or dead, or actual events is purely coincidental.

The views and opinions expressed in this work are those of the author and do not necessarily reflect the views and opinions of Editio Publishing, LLC.

내 동생 건들면 너희는 다 죽은 목숨이다 by 몰포

This English edition was published by Editio Publishing LLC in 2025 by arrangement with GAHABOOKS c/o KCC (Korea Copyright Center Inc.), Seoul.

ISBN 978-1-959742-65-4 (Print)

Printed in the United States of America

https://editiopublishing.com/

Touch My Brother and You Die

CONTENTS

PART VII

LIFE #22 (ROSALITE, TWENTY YEARS OLD)

I had many busy days after I returned from the Crown Prince's palace.

I was always busy, but this was a completely different level of busy. A few days ago, my birthday dinner was held in the dining hall, but we only made one toast and then went back to work without eating anything. That was how busy we were.

The Crown Prince showed his willingness to meet with potential wives and get married. This was not the time to celebrate my birthday.

The current situation being as important as it was, the four duchies agreed to minimize personal celebrations for the time being. We were all busy contacting the royal families from different countries with whom we had connections.

The Roxburg family obviously supported the second princess of a larger royal family in the Commonwealth of Czerepia.

While I had surreptitiously mentioned the match would be favorable in terms of border protection, the fact was our family had a sisterhood with their city. We had no choice but to back them.

Stupid Theodore. Did you really think you could escape the evil claws of the duchies if you found a wife from a different country? If you really believe that, then you totally underestimated the power the dukes have in this kingdom.

More people wanted to board the ducal trains over the royal train than we could count, even from surrounding countries. *Like how making an appointment with Her Eminence the Pope is even more difficult than with the Emperor of the Largole Empire himself.*

Speaking of the pope... I should have made some business cards like Luke.

I'm so bitter that I couldn't give the pope my business card because our meeting was scheduled last minute! I guess it's mostly my fault that I didn't prepare beforehand. I mean, my name solves everything in our kingdom.

Still, how did it even slip my mind when I have such a great example like Luke Shatel? If I had left a card with the name Rosalite Roxburg on it, the pope would have contacted me the moment she needed something in relation to the kingdom. Accessibility is incredibly important. Stupid Rosalite!

I took one of Luke's business cards from my cardholder. He always included one whenever he sent me gifts and bribes. As I ogled and admired the card, I heard the news that Jack had arrived and got up from my chair.

Jack's jawbone hadn't yet healed from the strike he had received from Aster. But he could do simple tasks like making deliveries to the palace.

"Hurry, Jack! We need to be faster than the Edanellis!"

I stayed up all night for two days so I could introduce Princess Natalie of the Principality of Nimernia—which belonged to the Commonwealth of Czerepia—to the Crown Prince faster than anyone from the House of Edanelli.

Jack gazed sympathetically at the bags under my eyes and saluted to signal that he understood me. He then turned to Aster, making all sorts of gestures.

He whirled his fists around, raised his middle finger, and finished everything off by dragging a thumb across his throat. I guess he meant that he was going to kill her when he was better.

Aster did not show any change in her emotions. She simply replied with a "right back at you," which caused Jack to dive at her like he was going to kill her this instant and forced Lily to go through the trouble of separating them.

I'm amazed that Lily can entirely hold her own when she's up against Jack. What exactly is she?

"Little miss—!"

What now?

I had just coaxed Jack and sent him off to the palace, and now another man was banging at my office door.

It was a voice that I hadn't heard recently, but it was strangely familiar. A voice about two octaves lower than Jack's, yet oddly similar. Kind of like the princess' guard John's, but more thoughtless...

"Little miss!"

The man, who flung open the doors without my permission, was so tall and large that he almost had to bend in half to get through the doorframe.

He was sweating buckets in this chilly weather, which meant that he had run all the way here. The man standing in front of me, anxiously flailing his arms because he couldn't think of what he needed to say, was Jean Brown. I had sent him to Uncle Louis' marquisate to keep him away from Rion ages ago.

His build never ceases to surprise me. How tall is he again? Seven and a half feet?

His hands and feet were also enormous, and it seemed as though my entire head would fit in his palm.

"L-little miss! Lord Glen! Mom! Force! House!"

Is there some kind of emergency? Is that why he rushed over to the duke's estate without my permission?

I wondered what his business was and listened to his words carefully. Then, deducing something horrific had happened, I slammed my hand down onto my desk and yelled right back. "What? Marchioness Diamont kidnapped Glen and imprisoned him in the marquis' estate?!"

Jean nodded vigorously.

Wait, if Glen has been kidnapped, who's looking after the Veloce territory?

"What about the Veloce region? Who is in charge right now?"

"Philip! Diana!"

Those two are filling in for him. Thank goodness Glen made that emergency manual. They wouldn't have too much trouble managing the territory for now.

"How on earth did the marchioness capture Glen? Did she go to the Veloce region herself?"

"Lord Glen! Come! Mom's sick!"

Ugh. I told him not to go to the Diamont Marquisate, but I guess he just couldn't help himself. World's greatest son ever. Never have I seen one like him.

"Violet! Bring Rion here! Aster, you're coming with me to the marquisate!"

I'm going to Uncle Louis' house in the end. Is the marchioness actually an amazing tactician?

I suppose if she could drag Uncle Louis, with his deadpan eyes and absence of a human heart, into getting remarried, then she's something for sure.

"Jean!"

"Yes, little miss!"

"Close your eyes and turn around!"

"...Huh?"

God, you're already so slow, and now you're deaf, too?

When I told him that Rion was going to arrive soon, so he mustn't look, Jean slowly blinked his large cow-like eyes and uncharacteristically tried to defy my orders.

"Don't want to. Want to. See. Young master."

"If you look at him, I'll kick you out of the house!"

"Ha..."

Why are you acting so cute when you're as big as a barn!

My heart melted at the sight of Jean shuffling to the corner of my office, whimpering like a little puppy. I went after him and consoled him, explaining that I was doing this for him.

Throughout all my lives... Jean Brown always fell in love with Rion at first sight.

Every time. Ten out of ten. No, a thousand out of one hundred.

SIXTY-FOUR

Rion was a death trap for Jean, who was always obsessed with him and gave his all. And when Jean became nothing more than a fish in Rion's net, he was destined to be manipulated and abused until the day Rion died.

Rion was a kind, cute little kid, but he was strangely unusual when it came to dealing with Jean. After I ordered Jean to be Rion's guard in Life #4, he always had scratches and injuries on his body. Then, Rion was sent to a boarding school outside the capital, and I made Jean go along to serve him. Every time they came back during breaks, one part of Jean's body was always damaged or broken. After Rion was accepted into the royal knightage, which was famous for selecting people based on their looks, Jean fell ill with a lingering disease and passed away, even before Rion.

Whenever I left Jean with Rion in the lives that followed, Jean always ended up with some kind of problem. So, I did my best to keep them apart from then on. Nothing good ever came of the two meeting each other.

"Aster," I ordered. "Make sure that Jean does not turn around, even as a joke."

Word that Rion had arrived reached my ears, so I opened the door first and grabbed his face. *He's even taller! Now I have to stand on my tiptoes to reach his face.*

"Keep your eyes on me, Rion. There is no one in the corner of the room."

"Yes. No one in the corner."

What a good boy.

I told him my business as I stared into his eyes, still holding on to his face. Rion stared back with equal intensity, leaning forward as though he was going to fall into my eyes, before he whipped out a piece of paper.

"You have been requesting such business from me often these days, so I have prepared a contract."

"A contract?"

"Yes. It is good for you and good for me, and everyone will be happy."

No such thing exists!

Doubtful, I took the paper that Rion had prepared, reminding him once more: "Don't look away from me, Rion."

"Thank you very much."

Thank you very much...? Why?

I have no idea what you're talking about. But it's fine because you aren't even glancing at the corner where Jean Brown is. Good. This gives me time to read the contract.

The contents were quite simple.

As compensation for working in my place, Asterion Roxburg is to be appointed my official aide once his schooling is complete. I must give Asterion Roxburg the right to be my partner at official events, even if it is second to Glen Hoffen. I must lavish Asterion Roxburg with public displays of physical affection every day, including the days we fight. If such affections are pushed back due to business trips and so forth, I must show such affections in one setting, all at once.

That last clause has a lot of nitty-gritty details.

"What exactly do you mean by 'physical affection?'"

"From hugs to kisses."

"Fine."

You really like your warm hugs, don't you, Rion?

What he was asking for wasn't a big deal. I signed the contract and stamped it with the Roxburg seal before returning it to him. "You may break the contract anytime if you do not want me all over you anymore."

"That will never happen as long as I live."

No. It's because you haven't hit puberty yet. Just looking at me will be disgusting to you when you get older.

Of course, Asterion was obsessed with his sister, so he never showed any signs of distaste, but that could change as he grew older.

I'd know better if I got to see him live past his mid-twenties!

Just wait. Once you're past your mid-twenties, your sister will become gross, and your abnormal sister-obsession will finally end.

"I shall be back tomorrow at the latest," I told him. "Work well until then."

"Of course. There's been a rockslide at the Diamont Marquisate due to the recent rainfall, so please be careful."

"I will."

…

…Hm? Did I say that I was going to Uncle Louis' place?

Huh. I guess he heard from Violet on his way here.

I hurried, wanting to settle the matter quickly. After drafting up two copies of a specific consent form, I tied one to the leg of a carrier pigeon and sent it to Uncle Louis. I took the other one straight to the duke and got his stamp of approval.

I need to be well prepared to get Glen back.

I noticed Jean was still being led here and there by Aster with his hands over his eyes, so I told him he could open them and headed to the stables.

If there had been a landslide because of the rain, the road would obviously be tough. Riding in a carriage would take too long, so I had no choice but to go on horseback.

My horse, Elizabeth, can jump over any obstacle because she's excellent!

Oof... It would take forever to explain her pedigree. I'd have to start at the very beginning, since her ancestor of the previous-previous generation was a warhorse in the northernmost country of the Commonwealth of Czerepia. There wasn't anyone I could brag to, though.

Aster wouldn't be interested in something like this. Maybe I should talk to Jack one of these days.

Holding her reins tightly, I checked that a fully armed Aster was keeping pace, and I headed to Uncle Louis' estate, which was a thirty-minute ride. If things didn't work out, I would probably need Aster to use her strength.

Passing through the most crowded town in the marquisate, I headed further inward toward the forest.

An estate covered in twisting ivy appeared, grand and dreary as though it reflected Uncle Louis' character. *I can never tell what he's thinking behind his deadpan expression.*

Compared to him, the duke was practically bubbly. Even if his life motto was "Get to the point." Then again, he was aggressively enthusiastic whenever he had the opportunity to dance.

After handing Elizabeth's reins to the servants of the estate, I headed to Uncle Louis' office. On the way there, I ran into a familiar face.

The man seemed to have recognized me because he greeted me delightfully. "Welcome, young duchess. You arrived quicker than we expected."

"You could have given me a heads up if you knew I was going to rush over."

"Why would I bother when your servant does his job splendidly?"

The older yet respectful man was my cousin and the future marquis of the House of Diamont, Benjamin.

Ugh. He has eyes like a dead fish, too. It's creepy. Why does everyone in this family except Dylan have eyes like that?

"Are you to see my father before seeing the marchioness?"

"Why, do you have a problem with that?"

"Not at all. How could I dare to have a problem with the young duchess? I was just being inquisitive."

Yeah, you've always been curious about a lot of things. You put poisonous carrots on Dylan's plate just because you wanted to know if people would die when they ate them.

The worst part about Benjamin was that he had no malicious intent. When he gave Dylan the carrots in my previous life, he had no intention of killing him. He was truly curious about the effects of the poisonous carrots. The scariest part of that incident was when Dylan died. Benjamin said, "Oh? He really died?" and then acted like he never had a younger brother in the first place.

That was why Glen felt so threatened after he lost his buffer back then. Despite everything, Dylan was the only one protecting his family from Benjamin.

"I suppose you are tailing me because you are curious," I said.

"As expected, young duchess. You know me so well."

No, I don't! I don't know anything about you. Not a single thing.

Shaking my head, I avoided looking at him as best as I could before I arrived in front of my uncle's office and waited for the doors to open at my announcement.

I spent the wait ignoring Benjamin's unfunny jokes. Before long, the doors creaked open, and a middle-aged man who looked like the duke with dead eyes came into view.

He looked like he had done hard manual labor recently, because the skin under his eyes was just as dark and dead as his gaze. He glanced over the consent form I had sent by carrier pigeon and then ripped it to shreds right in front of me.

"I'm sorry," he said. "But I cannot consent to this."

"Why not?"

"Because it's no fun."

You and your fucking fun! That consent form was the quickest way to get Glen back! Don't you understand?

In that form, which the duke had already consented to, was my request to destroy a part of Uncle Louis' mansion to retrieve Glen. *It's my fault for thinking that Uncle Louis would just agree to it because we were all busy.*

It didn't cross my mind that getting Glen back would be about his damn entertainment.

"Benjamin."

"Yes, young duchess?"

"You know something, don't you?"

"I do."

"Any hope that you will tell me?"

"It will be a beautiful sight. The young duchess running around on her own two feet to figure it all out."

These assholes are obsessed with entertainment.

Pushing down the rage that welled up inside of me, I remembered that the duke and I were obsessed with dancing, so I tried to understand the two people.

Yeah, I guess they'd want to entertain themselves by toying with me if all they do is work like crazy.

"Jean Brown."

"Y-yes?"

"Where's Glen?"

"...Tower!"

Tower? Where the hell is that? There's a tower in the estate?

I had never seen such a building within the estate in any of my previous lives, so I hastily ran to the window in Uncle Louis' office and flung it open. Leaning forward as much as I could, I twisted my head left and right to find the tower. Aster grabbed my waist, telling me it was dangerous, so I was able to lean even farther to look around. A groan of horror escaped my lips when it came into view.

There really is a freaking tower.

"Has that building always been here?"

"We built it." The dead-eyed Marquis Diamont sidled up next to me and gazed at the tower proudly.

Yes, I can tell you made it, considering I never know what is going on in that head of yours. But why? Why did you make it? And Glen's up there? Is he Princess Glen now? Is he a princess trapped in a tower?

"Allow me to explain."

You look like you're having the time of your life, too, Benjamin.

As though reminiscing about a faraway past, the curious cat with silver hair closed his golden eyes. "It all began when the marchioness suggested that we test whether the young duchess is a compatible woman to be Glen Hoffen's wife."

"So?" Watching the heir of the Diamont Marquisate utter bullshit in such a serious manner made me realize exactly how bleak their future was.

"So, we built the tower."

"That's it?"

"Yes."

This is why Grandpa Roxburg said he had absolutely nothing to leave to that son of a bitch, Louis, and kicked him out of the main estate, to be penniless, before stashing him in the marquisate and forbidding him to step even one foot into the outside world.

SIXTY-FIVE

The only reason the marquisate developed so much was because my father, the duke, supported Uncle Louis once he had become the head of the house. Uncle Louis was the duke's only younger brother, after all.

The marquisate was just a rural area when Uncle Louis was first sent here. That was what I had heard from the duke.

"If you keep acting like this, the marquisate's only revenue will be the crops from your small estate garden."

"I like farming," Uncle Louis replied, "so it doesn't matter."

"We have already studied up on farming in case that was to happen, young duchess."

As I stood there, watching the two discuss preparations for their possible removal from the family register, I suddenly missed Dylan.

He would have made a proper noble had he not touched Rion. He was easy to handle because he only moved within my expectations.

"Now, young duchess," Uncle Louis said. "When you take a closer look at the tower, you will see that I myself was the one who set the cornerstone. Thus, I had the naming rights. That is why the name of the tower is...!"

"Is?"

"The Tower of Ordeals!"

I'm already in a pit of ordeals because of you, and now I have to go through even more? Where the hell is the marchioness? It'll be easier to straighten things out with her.

"Where is Marchioness Diamont?"

"She's waiting for you at the top of the tower, young duchess."

"You should have seen the way she kept refusing to stay in a place so cramped and dirty."

Wait, what? I think I just heard something important.

At Uncle Louis' careless comment, I came to my senses. Darting my eyes between the tower and my uncle, I realized who had been pulling the strings all along.

"Don't tell me the fit that the marchioness threw was just an excuse for you to have fun?"

"..."

"Go on, tell me. Because things are falling into place right now. There is no way this situation would have come this far, no matter how angry she was. You lent her a hand and then you took it to another level, didn't you?"

The marquis and his son are both pretending they can't hear me with the same faces. Christ, even the way they're playing innocent is the same.

My mind went blank. Tears pricked my eyes because I felt so bad for Glen, who had been forcibly dragged into these two people's playpen. *I feel kind of bad for the marchioness, too. Just a little bit. Yes, she dug her own grave, but it's sad that she was caught up in their games.*

"Fine. I'll go. I'll go up the tower, okay?"

I sighed deeply, and the two followed me as I left the room, looking as delighted as anything. *I need to make preparations to remove these two from the family register the moment I get home.*

"Why are you following me, Uncle Louis? Aren't you busy this time of day?"

"I can work overnight. I am not about to miss out on this exciting event."

"You must have too much free time."

"You Roxburgs should know just how much time I have. Your grandfather and father were the ones who threatened me never to leave the marquisate."

"You simply reaped what you sowed. You're the one who shoved the duke into a reservoir, knowing full well that he couldn't swim."

Right. That's why Grandpa Roxburg flew into a rage and put surveillance on Uncle Louis so he could never leave the marquisate.

The order remained in place even after grandpa retired, and the duke became the head. The marquis could not leave the marquisate unless the duke gave him permission.

He sometimes came to the capital when there was a mandatory royal or household event. He could also leave his estate if the duke felt like it. Every time he was allowed to leave, he would stick to the duke like a dismal shadow and gloomily ask him to lift his house arrest since he was remorseful.

"But... I was so curious," Uncle Louis replied. "I wanted to see if the distinguished Edward would instinctively learn how to swim if he fell into the water."

"Right. What you mean to say is that you were curious to see if he would die when he fell into the water."

"My niece knows me so well!"

No! I swear to God, I don't know what the fuck goes on inside your heads!

Wait... did Dylan force Glen onto that horse because he was curious to see if Glen would die when he fell off? No, it couldn't be.

Dylan was different from those two. I really don't want to believe that the three of them were the same.

"Haha..."

With a train of people following me, I arrived at the foot of the tower. It was five stories high and very poorly constructed. Benjamin's handwriting had been carved into a brick near the bottom.

It's called the Tower of Ordeals as he said, but the construction date was exactly two months ago. It's totally jerry-built!

"Are you sure this is safe? It won't come crashing down on my way up?"

Stop pretending you can't hear me and answer my questions!

Both of them followed me inside, so I figured that the tower wouldn't collapse, but I was still apprehensive.

Whatever they used to cement the bricks together is crumbling! That would never happen if it were built by professionals. Please don't cave in until I bring Glen safely outside.

"There's nothing here."

Aside from the shitty construction, the Tower of Ordeals didn't live up to its name. There was nothing on the first floor, or the second floor either. Aster was walking in front of me just in case, so the lack of anything dangerous in the tower was almost embarrassing.

"You'll see when you get up there." Uncle Louis snickered.

Yeah. There's definitely something. Look at Uncle Louis and Benjamin giggling. Is this fun? Is this entertaining for them?

"Little miss."

Did something finally appear?

At Aster's cautious tone, I calmly scanned my surroundings. *Is that a door she's pointing at...?*

Why the hell is it made out of stone? Does it even move?

"If you want to take Glen, you have to be strong."

"That's right, young duchess. The marchioness had us create this test door. She won't allow the marriage if you can't carry Glen out of the tower in your arms."

I knew you two were behind this.

They probably created the door to make this difficult for me, but Aster was never a child to be respectful of other people's intentions. She marched forward and put her hands on the door.

When she pushed forcefully, the door moved backward, raising up a cloud of dust and powdered stone. Uncle Louis and Benjamin threw a fit, raging that the test wasn't for Aster.

*I wasn't going to say anything, but the way this installation is moving... it's totally a rip-off of Hun*** × Hun***, isn't it? It's totally ***ter × ***ter!*

"It's fine, Aster. I'll do it."

"Yes, little miss."

If they want someone strong to be Glen's wife, it's only right that I do this myself. It wouldn't be strange for assassins to appear once he becomes the husband of a duchess.

The hell...? Now that I think about it, it's completely appropriate for the marchioness to bring up this condition. I guess she was scared that Glen would die as well, since she did say she "lost two of her sons" because of me.

Even though she preferred Dylan to Glen, a mother is still a mother. Yeah, she's entrusting her precious son to me. Showing her that I can do this isn't a problem.

Excusing myself, I returned to the first floor to cast an enhancement spell. I discovered a rebar lying around and bent it in half to check my muscular strength.

I had updated and improved this spell ever since my encounter with the giant squid in order to lessen the side effects. *I only have to suffer from deadly muscle pain for one day now!*

Despite the astronomical cost of keeping him at the estate, Sir Sage had been a great help. I would have never improved my magic if I had to struggle on my own.

Right. I'm all set now. Let's go.

After tossing the rebar away, I went back upstairs to the entrance of the second floor and made people stand back. I positioned myself the way Aster had done, and with a hard push, the door began to scrape backward...

Hold up. My physical strength is similar to Aster's even with my enhancement spell? I was hoping it would be a whole lot more dramatic!

"Magnificent work, little miss."

"Little miss! Magnificent!"

Aster and Jean looked excited at what I had done and were clearly impressed.

Jean patted me proudly as he marveled at how strong I had become, but Uncle Louis and Benjamin had both taken three steps back, looking sour.

"...I forgot that you are related to *her*."

"Is the young duchess a human or a gorilla?"

"Why don't you two stop complaining and continue to the next test?" I snapped. "I'm a busy person."

We're all busy people here. Why are we doing this? Well, I know it's because you two are psychopaths who are crazy about toying with people. I resolved to enforce their house arrest when I got back home.

So! What's the next task?

"Benjamin!"

"Yes?!"

Wow. Just look at how they brighten up at the thought of their next little game.

Excitedly scurrying to the second floor, the two men readied the next task to fuck me over as though they had no fear of me.

Let's see... The second floor doesn't seem as empty as the first. There was a grand piano smack dab in the middle of the room and a table off to the side with a red buzzer resting on top. Several chairs sat behind it.

*I've seen that buzzer on A*T.*

"You can't get married if you can't sing!" Uncle Louis shouted.

Oh God, that scared me.

While I had been looking around the room, Uncle Louis pressed the red buzzer and instructed me to sing well if I wanted to take Glen back.

*Yeah... I've seen that buzzer on A*T.*

"You know how they say you need to 'sing for your supper'? It's time to 'sing for your marriage' on the stage we created! My son Benjamin volunteered to accompany you on the piano."

"Although you'll disown me if my playing is unsatisfactory."

Highly amused by their own incomprehensible banter, both men guffawed. Benjamin then warmed up with a piece that sounded like it was from *Czerny One Hundred Progressive Studies* and banged his fingers down in a tonic chord. He pressed me to hurry up and choose a song.

Is he confident that he can play any song I choose?

"Well... then..."

I'll play it safe and sing that cool jazz song that's popular these days.

It was kind of embarrassing to have to sing in front of all these people. But I decided to be brave because Aster and Jean were zealously cheering for me. I sang as best as I could and turned to Uncle Louis.

The man painstakingly pondered for a moment and then flatly pressed the buzzer.

"Why? I sang the whole song!"

"Your singing lacks soul."

Soul?! Are you kidding me?

I wanted to give up and just take the whole tower down, but Aster lunged at Uncle Louis, grabbing for his throat as she shouted something about how she couldn't let anyone who insulted my singing live, even a relative. So, I hastily started singing a different song.

When Aster fucks shit up, she does it colossally. As I rushed into song to distract Aster, Benjamin reacted quickly and accompanied me on the piano. Seeing that, Aster docilely took her seat again and clapped to the beat.

Whew. If Aster punched Uncle Louis, he'd probably die.

CHAPTER
SIXTY-SIX

Uncle Louis said I didn't have enough soul. I'll sing whatever I want then. At my fast-paced dance song, Jean stood up and clapped his hands as though he were watching a grandchild perform in a talent show.

This is going to work! I don't know what "soul" is, but this song made someone happy. You could say that I moved him emotionally. And what does that mean? It means I touched their soul!

My song is moving and soulful! I whipped around to face my uncle as I finished the last verse. He stared at me with his dead eyes as he pondered again and then mercilessly pressed the buzzer.

"What now?!"

"I felt the soul, but your singing is not as good as the piano!"

Why the hell are you so harsh? Does my singing have to be out of this world to get married?! Why is getting married so hard?! And stop raising your nose high in the air like you're so pleased with yourself, Benjamin! You're pissing me off!

Fine. I'll sing the national anthem. I have no choice but to sing it. A citizen of the kingdom can't nitpick at its soulfulness, and it's simple, so the piano won't outshine me.

I began singing the song that praised our beautiful country, and Uncle Louis' face immediately darkened with boredom. He smacked the buzzer before I even finished.

Okay, let's hear the reason this time.

"Rosalite. You keep singing with your head. Glen would never! You need to sing with your abdomen."

I see. I get it. You don't intend to let me pass.

I truly understand that you're trapped in this marquisate with no entertainment whatsoever. I spent some time playing your little games because our duchy also tosses a lot of work your way, and I'm grateful that you work hard. But enough is enough.

"Aster!"

"Yes, little miss?"

"Smash everything! I'll take full responsibility!"

"Yes, little miss!"

That's the happiest she's been all day. Why did I even hold back when this was precisely the reason I brought her along in the first place? I mean, I did want to take Glen home as quietly as possible because there's no telling what these two will do to him if I rub them the wrong way. But that would be solved if I reinforced their house arrest arrangement when I got back home.

"Stand back, little miss. It's dangerous." Aster shifted her stance in front of the large, padlocked door and emanated her aura. She pulled back her heavy longsword with one arm and stretched the other to guide the tip of her blade, then she charged the door with a battle cry.

"Die, William Brown!"

Is... your aura activated by your rage against your father or something...?

Her blade hit its mark at the center of the padlock, and the entire door exploded in a cloud of sawdust like it had been drilled right through.

The force of it was terrifying. *No wonder the giant squid died with a single blow.*

"Let's go up, little miss."

"Huh? Oh, right, yeah."

I'm so glad she's my guard. I would've been scared shitless if she wasn't on my side.

When I followed Aster to the third floor, I saw piles of food ingredients and kitchen appliances. *Looks like they want to see if I can cook. I'm seeing two cutting boards laid out, so I guess they want me to compete with someone. Who the hell wanted to cook?*

"Die, Jack Brown!"

Oh, your aura works with that phrase, too. I see. She can just activate her aura when she's pissed. Rage power-up, right? I've seen this trope many times.

I grabbed my skirts to run faster and passed through the fourth floor, which held a spinning wheel and knitting needles. I would have stayed here the whole month if I had done as Uncle Louis said. Just busting up the place was the right thing to do.

"Glen! Are you there? Stand away from the door. It's dangerous!" Shouting from the entrance of the fifth floor, I made Aster smash the door.

When I stepped inside, I saw a room that appeared lived-in and fairly well-furnished. It wasn't tiny or dirty like the marchioness had allegedly claimed. It appeared to be well-stocked with food, too.

The reason the room looked livable was because a dead-eyed Glen was sitting on the carpeted floor, eating an apple while playing with his little brother.

"L-Lady Rosalite...?"

The apple he was munching on fell onto the thick, fluffy carpet. *You look so relaxed while I've been busting my ass to save you?*

"H-how did you get here, Lady Rosalite?"

"I heard that you were imprisoned, so I came to save you."

"Huh? Imprisoned? Me?"

The hell? Is he not even aware of that?

I told Glen about his mother's wicked schemes to lure him here and lock him in the tallest room of the tower, and how Jean came to get me.

He looked startled and defended his mother. "No, you have it all wrong, Lady Rosalite. It's not uncommon for mother to lock me in my room. She's done it frequently ever since I was young."

"...What?"

"She also left me behind in crowded places and went home by herself, or accidentally threw my plate of food on the floor or made me stay home by myself while she took Dylan out for the day."

Christ. I'm sorry. Please stop. Even Cinderella probably wasn't as abused as you were.

But Glen truly didn't think the situation was urgent and told me about his day, describing how fun it had been to hang out with his mother and play with his little brother.

Well... as long as you had fun...

"Where is Marchioness Diamont?" I asked. "I thought she was with you."

"Oh, she went over to where the water fountain is."

Huh, they built a lot of good stuff despite the shitty construction.

Ordering the others not to follow me, I headed toward the area the marchioness had fled to with a hard expression on my face. Unlike Glen, the marchioness was filthy from being locked up in the tower for the day. She flinched when she saw me.

"I-I see you've come, Rosalite."

"I'll be brief."

If it weren't for Glen, I'd have no reason to leave Jean here to protect the marchioness and her child from Benjamin. That fact needed to be hammered into her head.

"Bother me or Glen again and you're dead."

"My, Rosalite, are you threatening me? If Glen hears about thi—"

"Sure. Tell him. You'll still be dead afterward."

Letting out a deep sigh, I turned away from the marchioness, who looked like she was itching to say more, and walked toward my uncle and Benjamin. I had no more business here now that I had rescued Glen.

"Uncle Louis. Your house arrest will be confined to the estate grounds, so prepare yourself. Benjamin, you too will never be allowed to step one foot outside the marquisate.

Jean, bring Glen. Please monitor the marquis' estate closely, as always."

I need to take Glen and get out of this cesspit of would-be criminals.

Uncle Louis and Benjamin were squawking about something behind me. But I ignored them and headed down the tower, ordering Aster to bring Elizabeth. When my horse arrived, I helped Glen sit on her back first.

Climbing behind him, I held him tightly with one arm and took the reins in my other hand. As I wordlessly steered Elizabeth, Glen fidgeted in my arms, glancing at me anxiously as he had been doing since we left the fifth floor of the tower.

"Uhm... Lady Rosalite? Are... are you mad?"

"Yes."

I'm mad because you ignored my advice and came all the way to this place because of your "sick" mom. I'm mad because my asshole relatives took you hostage so they could play one of their stupid games. I'm mad because I don't know what the hell I should do with you when you smile like an idiot and love that woman despite the abuse just because she's your mother.

You mean so much to me and the duke, so how could any of us be pleased when you meekly obey summons from someone else's house?

There was a lot that I wanted to say but didn't know how, so I just sat there in silence, frowning. Glen curled up, disheartened.

This won't do. I'm just venting my anger on you. And I'm worried that you might fall off the horse again if you try to move away from me.

"Hold on tight, or you'll fall." I made him put his arms around my shoulders and pulled him closer to me by his waist before spurring Elizabeth into a gallop.

Glen didn't say anything and fidgeted a bit longer before he leaned his body into mine, nodding once.

I wish you'd always listen to what I tell you.

The situation had been settled earlier than I expected, and we arrived at the duke's estate around sunset.

I'll be able to report what happened at the marquisate while I have dinner with the duke, and then get a swift order of reinforcement for the terms of the house arrest.

My hatred toward the Diamonts grew bigger than ever as I asked Aster to help Glen off the horse and to escort him to his room.

Someone I had been seeing a lot lately came into view at the front entrance.

"Welcome back, sister." Rion, who had been working in my place, came out to greet me as though he had been waiting. Apparently still following my orders from earlier to keep his eyes on me, Rion ignored Glen and Aster and came up close. "You haven't shown me today's worth of physical affection yet. I was waiting for your return."

Oh, right. I was in a hurry earlier.

It's the first day of the contract. I can't be breaching it already.

I patted away the dust on my clothes to be courteous, while Rion stood with his arms spread wide. I gave a warm hug, patted him on the back, and then kissed his cheek as a little extra thanks.

I can't believe he works in my place just for this reward. How convenient.

"Lady Rosalite...?"

Huh? Why are you still here?

As I was about to go look for the duke after fulfilling my contract duties, Glen's bitter voice floated toward me. Pointing rudely, he stared back and forth at me and Rion and expressed his curiosity about what just happened. Rion pulled out the contract like he had prepared for this beforehand and shoved it in Glen's face.

"These acts are a reward for working in my sister's place. Do you have a problem with it?"

"You are planning to do this every day...?"

"Of course. By the way, we will also be working in the same room soon. I will appreciate your guidance."

Haha, Rion is so well-mannered.

Rion bowed and held out his hand for a handshake. But strangely enough, Glen smacked it away and said he was going inside first because he needed to think about something alone.

I wonder if he's horse-sick because he isn't used to riding horseback.

"What is the matter with him?" Rion asked. "Is he horse-sick or something?"

"Hmm... it appears so..."

"I simply offered a friendly handshake. It hurts my heart that he rejected it. Did I do something wrong?"

"No. What would you have done wrong? Glen has gone through a lot today, so just think that he's had a rough day."

Even acts of kindness are annoying when you feel emotionally and physically sick.

Rion stuck to my side, linking his arm in mine, and I told him what a cute, good boy he was on the way to find the duke. When I found the duke, I requested that he reinforce Uncle Louis' house arrest order and issue a new one for Benjamin as well.

The duke accepted my request and told me that he would give his formal consent when I turned in an official request form. He then stared uncomfortably at Asterion, who was still clinging to me with his head on my shoulder.

"Aren't you two a little too close?"

"Are we?"

"No, Your Grace," Rion said. "This is normal between brother and sister."

Uh... is it?

I've personally never seen a brother and a sister act like this before. But if Rion says it's normal, then I guess that's true. He has no reason to lie.

The duke seemed suspicious as well, but as he couldn't find a reason why Rion would lie about that, he nodded and didn't bring it up again.

Rion sat next to me and enjoyed a delicious dinner since he was in the dining hall anyway, and then coquettishly told me he wanted something for his coming birthday.

I don't know what it is that you want, but if you're willing to act like that so you can get it, I guess buying it for you would be the right thing to do.

I told him to tell me whatever he wanted. Ecstatic, Rion said that he would bring me a list soon.

He's going to rip a hole in my wallet.

CHAPTER
SIXTY-SEVEN

Four days had passed since I brought Glen home with me, but he did not return to the Veloce region. He said that he would stay and help me for a few days since he was already at the estate, and we had been working together in my office ever since. His attitude was the same as always, but I felt strangely uncomfortable.

What exactly is this feeling? It's like he's glaring at me from where I can't see him. Whenever Rion barged in with snacks, Glen would bang his cane on the floor threateningly and tell him not to interfere, as the adults were working.

I wish he'd tell me if he has something on his mind. It's not like I won't listen to what he has to say.

Glen's bad mood would worsen at the mention of Rion. I wondered if there was a problem between the two, when I was suddenly lifted into the air.

"There's a royal carriage, little miss."

Aster! You've finally learned!

Aster lifted me into her arms to bolt downstairs, and I held on to her tightly as she jumped straight down to the first floor. I felt fear grip the pit of my stomach in a moment of zero gravity and braced myself.

We landed with a resounding *boom*, and I saw the duke rushing over from far away. I was way faster than he was this time.

I kind of feel bad for saying this, but uh… based on the reaction time, I think… well, perhaps it's time for Sir William to, you know… retire…?

"We've arrived, little miss."

Whoa, already? If I remember correctly, you couldn't beat Sir William when it came to speed. You've grown so much, Aster.

Feeling a bit emotional, I accepted the messages from the royal palace. As I sifted through them, I was disappointed to realize there wasn't anything that looked like an invitation to a banquet. However, there was other good news I had been waiting for, so I called the duke and relayed the information to him.

"Your Grace, it looks like the Crown Prince is finally going to meet with a marriage prospect."

The duke was probably waiting for this news, too. Who did the little prince choose to meet first? Which family recommended her?

Inwardly praying for it to be Princess Natalie from Nimernia, I opened up the sheepskin parchment and saw a name I had never even heard of, written underneath the date of the meeting.

"Who is Irini Mikeah…?"

Unable to find the name in my mental database, I turned to the duke, who had the greater database, and information about the woman came forth from his mouth.

"Irini Mikeah. The eighth princess of the Largole Empire. She probably turned eighteen this year."

Why though…?

Once again unable to find a reason why the Crown Prince would make this kind of decision, I turned to the duke for his guidance, and he answered without pause.

"He does not like the four duchies. He has most likely realized that all the candidates we brought to him have a connection with each of us."

"Impossible. His Highness is not that smart."

"You always underrate the Crown Prince's intelligence for some reason, Rosalite."

"Well, yes, because what would a child like him even know?"

"You are younger than him." The duke smiled one of his rare smiles and gently rapped my head with his knuckles.

At that, a small scuffle ensued between Aster and Sir William. Aster had instinctively gone into attack mode when the duke rapped me on the head, and Sir William had noticed.

He unleashed his wrath on his daughter by whacking her on the back of the head. "Have you lost your senses? He is the master of this house."

"I've... made a mistake."

Why would you do that, Aster? He's my father...

Only when I bowed low and apologized to the duke—because it was fully my fault for not educating Aster well—did she follow suit, looking regretful.

I'm happy she's become so strong in this life, but it's concerning that she's ready to bite anyone's head off. I should take Jack with me to official events or bring him along if I decide to take Aster.

"Keep her in line for just a little longer," the duke said. "This place will soon be yours anyway."

"You still have at least ten years until retirement, Your Grace."

"Ten years go by quick enough."

Not for me, they don't. I've been alive for decades, but the ten years that pass so easily for everyone else don't for me.

I swallowed my tears and told the duke I would be waiting eagerly for his retirement. He excitedly told me about how he had already bought an entire beach in the southern Edanelli Duchy and was building another estate. Clearly, he had already made detailed plans for his life after he gave the duchy to me.

I hope all your dreams come true, Your Grace. I told him soullessly and then steered the conversation back to the Crown Prince. We spoke at length about what we needed to do.

I felt bad for Theodore, but as Roxburgs, we could not stand by and watch the future king of the Alain Kingdom successfully get together with a princess from the Largole Empire.

Crown Prince. You. Must. Get. Married. To. Princess Natalie.

The duke and I put our heads together to find ways to disrupt the Crown Prince's meeting with the princess.

In the end, it was decided that I would be the one to get in the way of Imperial Princess Irini and the Crown Prince's meeting. Since we heirs were less busy than the dukes, we had a little competition to determine who would get to go and relax...

...Uhm, I mean, take on the mission, and I won.

The competition took place on a quiet night in Shatel Spa Land, located on the outskirts of the Roxburg territory.

Because there were only three heirs to the four duchies, I, Lady Rosalite of the House of Roxburg, met with Lady Dorothy of the House of Edanelli and Lord Anton of the House Vienarre at the hot springs. We spent some time hanging out after a nice bath and finally got down to business when it was nearly midnight.

After some discussion about what type of competition would be fair for all three of us, we agreed upon an indoor archery match. None of us were very physically strong and we'd never learned to shoot arrows before, so we figured this would be the fairest game to play.

We had Luke prepare targets, bows, and arrows, and I had the hardest time trying to push down my laughter as the three of us took aim.

Dummies! Challenging a former Korean to an archery match!

However, Lord Anton showed unexpected skill in hitting bullseyes, possibly due to his Vienarre genes. Lady Dorothy took about three shots before giving up, but Lord Anton fought so well that I almost lost. I was only able to win with the most points because Jack sneakily sabotaged the game. Lord Anton later complained to me and insultingly called me a "shady Roxburg."

No, wait, that's not an insult. Shady is the best praise for a Roxburg!

I bowed deeply to thank him for the compliment and for letting me win, teasing him, and then headed off to the baths again with Lady Dorothy to take another dunk before bed.

And so, the sands of time flew by.

"I'm sorry, an island?"

Yep, Rion.

The royal private island of Rioka, to be exact. Located about three miles northeast of the Vienarre tourist harbor, the island had beautiful white sand and was rumored to have an amazing underwater view due to the coral reef colonies.

And it's the place that the Crown Prince himself chose to have his marriage meeting.

"You are going to an island, where ships only come and go twice a day, to spend the night with the Crown Prince?"

"Don't say that in such a weird way, Rion. The Crown Prince's servants, my guards, and an imperial princess of the Largole Empire will be there as well."

"Whatever the case, you would still be sleeping under the same roof as the Crown Prince, wouldn't you?"

"That is correct."

"You cannot."

"I can."

"You cannot!"

I can, though.

The duke already gave me permission. I beat the other heirs not-so-fair-and-square in a challenge, and even my fiancé is working in the side office without saying anything about it. So, why are you getting your panties in a bunch?

I decided to take a little break now that Rion had arrived at my office as ordered. I had Lily prepare tea and snacks, while I called for Glen to join us.

Rion kept harping on about how I couldn't go to the island, so I had Glen sit down next to me and I poked him in the ribs to get him to take my side. But the man looked highly displeased and said the same thing as Rion.

"You cannot."

"Not you too, Glen."

"Because he's a man and you're a woman."

"You really like telling me that, don't you?"

"Lady Dorothy is the best suited for this job. Send her instead."

"No."

"Why do you even ask for my opinion if you're just going to do what you want?!"

Why are you mad at me again?

Glen barked at me as he usually did, and I hastily covered my ears.

Asterion, who was sitting opposite us, crossed his legs elegantly and spoke in a sweet voice. "Are you all right, sister? You're too harsh, Lord Glen. Why would you lash out at her like that? Look at how you have startled my sister."

"Piece of garbage," Glen muttered.

"What did you just say...?"

"I did not say anything," Glen replied. "My leg suddenly stopped working one day. Did something similar happen to your ears?"

"Did you hear what he said, sister? That man just insulted me!"

What... Huh? I can't really hear anything because my ears are plugged. Did Glen say something?

After I told Rion that I didn't hear anything, Glen laughed softly and took my hands in his to lower them from my ears, telling me it was nothing.

Well, if Glen says it's nothing, then it's nothing!

"Ugh!"

"You really like making that noise, don't you, Rion?"

"In any case, I am against it!" Rion pouted. "Why do you have to go? You cannot!"

"My bags are packed already. I summoned you here today so you can take over my work while I'm gone."

"If you are going only to sabotage the meeting, then I can handle it. I shall go in your stead."

"Never even think about it." I glared at him for the horrifying words he had uttered, and Rion closed his mouth tightly.

CHAPTER
SIXTY-EIGHT

Rion squirmed fretfully like a dog who needed to pee, attempting to read my expression. He asked me if I was angry, and I shook my head after a moment of contemplation.

More like surprised, not angry.

"That is a relief. I thought I did something wrong..."

"Wrong? No, you're doing a wonderful job. And who cares if you make some mistakes? Everyone makes mistakes. If you do something wrong outside of the estate, I'll sweep it under the rug for you."

"Thank you! You're the best."

"Yep. Just leave everything to your one and only sister."

"In that case, you have not given me today's worth of physical affection."

I didn't?

I supposed I didn't when I thought about it, so I moved to sit next to Rion. I gave him a day's worth of hugs, stretched his cheeks because he was so cute, and rubbed his back a few times.

When all of that was done, I realized that Rion had moved my teacup from its original location across the table to where I was sitting now.

"Here you go," he said. "Open up."

And he's even feeding me some of his cake. What a nice little boy. That's the part with the strawberry on top. You can have mine, too.

"You need to eat fruit to grow tall and strong," I told him. "Don't give me all of them. Have some strawberries."

"If you say so."

Look at him eating. Is he an angel? Is Rion actually an angel? How does this sweet child eat in such a pleasant way? Yes, little kids need to eat well when they're growing, even if the result is the mysterious Asterion.

"Rion will help while I am gone, but you have full authority, Lord Glen. I will leave everything in your hands."

"Fine, I can see you will do what you want even if I try to stop you. Will you take Aster as your guard?"

"Uhm... about that..."

I think I need to take Jack along.

Considering how she almost attacked the duke the other day, I needed someone to hold Aster's leash even when I wasn't there. *Jack is the perfect candidate for that.* Glancing sideways at him, I mentioned that I was planning to take them both.

Jack, who had been standing meekly to the side, suddenly spoke up. "I think it's best that I stay here, little miss."

"Oh, you can talk again? Congratulations, Jack."

"I've been able to talk the whole time. The doctor advised that I should keep my mouth shut if I wanted my bones to stick faster, so that's what I did."

"What a relief it is to see that you listen to what the doctor tells you. Good boy, Jack."

I wanted to take a look at his jaw as I was praising him, but I couldn't hold his face because his gas mask was in the way.

I ordered him to take off the ridiculous mask and put down the bladed weapons he held in both hands, but he refused, vehemently shaking his head.

"No way, little miss. There are too many people in this room."

"What does that have to do with taking off your gas mask?"

"If I take this off, then I have to breathe in the air that these folks breathe out."

...Are you a germaphobe, too...? Actually, no, Jack is probably more obsessive-compulsive...

"Anyhow, let me stay." Jack continued. "What would Lord Glen do without me?"

"What does Glen have to do with it?"

I gazed at Glen, confused, and for some reason, he shyly told Jack that he was going to be okay.

The hell? When did they get so close? Why are you being so sweet to my guard when I'm right here, Lord Hoffen?

"I won't lose anymore, Jack. Please don't worry about me and go along."

"Do you think the little snake sucked on his thumbs while you got stronger? Please listen to me, Lord Glen."

"Well, if you are that anxious... Why don't I call for Fraude to stay with me?"

"Hmm..."

Jack mused, ruffling the hair on the back of his head, and then nodded. "I understand. I suppose Fraude is better at handling these things than I am."

What are you two talking about? I asked Jack out of curiosity, but he just scoffed and went to hone the blades of his daggers.

"You'll never know, little miss."

Hey! Don't single me out!

As I huffed in frustration and stomped on the floor, Glen smiled as if he was trying to comfort me. He told me not to worry about the estate and to think of my excursion as a little vacation.

Hmph. Jack, I'll let you off easy this time because of Glen.

"You always take on so much work because of me, Lord Glen. I'm sorry... and thank you."

"It is all right. It's my job as your advisor, after all. But more than that..."

Hm? More than what? Why are you fidgeting again?

"How are our wedding preparations coming along?" he asked.

The tea I'd been drinking went up my nose. "Ahem! Ahem!" I managed to keep myself dignified, but I felt like I was going to die.

Oh my God, I totally forgot because of the whole Crown Prince's marriage thing!

Clearing my throat, I surreptitiously wiped the bit of tea trickling from my nostrils and decided to play dumb to get out of the office as fast as I could.

I have a lot to prepare, you know? Yes. That's why I need to get out as fast as I can. I'm not trying to avoid responsibility for forgetting about the preparations for my own marriage. Of course not.

I gave some vague excuse about business I had to attend to outside, took Jack with me, and raced to the duke's study. I found all the documents on Roxburg-style weddings and carried the pile back to my room, where I stuffed them into the trunk I had packed for the trip to the island.

Jack muttered and grumbled about how pathetic I was, but he also promised to keep it a secret from Glen and helped me pack.

I swear, you're such a nice boy, despite your look.

The day of the Crown Prince's meeting with his marriage prospect has finally come!

The weather was sunnier than I had expected, so I put on a straw hat and stole a pair of sunglasses from Jack's collection. Then, I had all our luggage loaded into two carriages, and my guards and I headed to the Vienarre tourist harbor.

It's still fall, but the sky is so clear and sunny! The sun is warm, and the breeze is nice and cool, too. It's like a summer day. I would have packed a swimsuit if I knew the weather was going to be like this. I heard the coral reefs are famous over there.

"Don't run, little miss!" Jack warned. "You're going to hurt yourself!"

How can I not run when the weather is so amazing? Do you even know how many months it's been since I left my office dungeon and got some sun, Jack?

As I ran about, spreading my arms wide to soak up the sun and giggling happily, I saw Theodore the Smiling Face climb down from his royal carriage.

I quickly dashed over to where he was and gave him my greetings, holding my straw hat firmly in the sea breeze.

"My, if it isn't the lady of the Roxburg duchy?" he greeted me sardonically. "I thought you were just a little commoner girl in that garb."

"You're wearing a lot of clothing for this warm weather, Your Highness. Are you sure you're not sweating from every swaddled pore? Why don't you lift up your arms so I can check?"

"My sweat glands know how to read the room, unlike you, Lady Rosalite. They are not as unmanageable as you are. I'm sure your fiancé would say something if he saw you prancing around with so much skin showing just because you are warm."

"My fiancé is kind and sweet, unlike you, Your Highness. So, he only tells me nice things."

"Is he on such a tight leash already? That poor man."

"As will be your future if this meeting goes well, Your Highness."

"Hmph. There is no way I would let that happen."

You asshole. Look at him whip his head around and leave for the ship without saying goodbye.

I shook my fist at the back of his head and collected Aster and Jack to board the ship as well.

The eighth princess of the Largole Empire had requested the meeting first, so the imperial side promised to let the Crown Prince bring as many servants and guards as he wanted and ensured the imperial princess brought as few people as possible.

Since they had yielded this much, it would have been rude for the Crown Prince to deny their request for a meeting. Besides, the imperial princess really seemed to like him.

According to the Roxburg informants in the royal palace, Princess Irini had written a letter to him directly, begging him to please meet with her just once, because she had admired him for such a long time.

Well... I mean...

It's possible for someone to be attracted to His Highness because his face on its own is splendid. She'll probably see how nauseating he is after she speaks with him a few times. Hm? I might not even have to do anything this time.

I really hope so. I just want to enjoy my vacation.

I went out to the bow of the ship to feel the breeze, and the island came into view. It was only three miles from the tourist port, so we landed shortly after, and the luggage was moved to the royal villa under my instruction and that of the Crown Prince's head servant. We worked together even better than I had imagined, and the luggage and people were put in their respective places sooner than any of us expected. Not wanting to miss this opportunity, I dragged the head servant to a remote location to recruit him for the Roxburgs.

Jack, who had been standing in the garden of the villa on the lookout for members of the royal palace, suddenly shouted. "Little miss! There's a big sailboat with imperial flags coming down onto the pier!"

Already? When exactly did they start sailing in order to get here at this time? Last night? They've been sailing nonstop since last freaking night?

Fascinated, I ran out to the garden and saw something even more fascinating.

What the hell is up with the lenses on Jack's gas mask? No wonder he just handed over his sunglasses. He brought a gas mask with a new function.

The lenses stretched out and retracted like a spyglass, and it seemed they magnified objects like one as well.

The only person who could make something like that was Sir Sage. I did see Jack on a one-man strike in front of the Magical Research Facility, demanding a new 007 apparatus because he's my guard. *Did he get that spyglass gas mask then?*

"Should we go, little miss?"

"Yeah. Greeting them down there would be the proper thing to do."

A road led to the villa, but it wound upward onto high ground, so they would have a difficult time getting up here unless they brought a carriage from the empire.

Theodore the Smiling Face ... is probably taking a nap right now.

I can't let the imperial princess know about the embarrassment of the kingdom, so I'll need to play for time.

Once we hitched the horses to a well-managed carriage, we quickly drove down to the pier to greet the eighth Imperial Princess.

CHAPTER
SIXTY-NINE

I really wanted to see what kind of entertainingly psychotic person would be in love with the Crown Prince, so I hopped off the carriage with a big smile plastered on my face. It soon crumpled when I saw the man holding the imperial princess' bags.

"Bleurgh!"

The baggage carrier was none other than Prince Lukius.

"It's rude to react that way upon seeing someone's face."

"I wasn't informed that you would be joining us, Prince Lukius."

"Well, I'm not here on official business. I'm simply here to carry the princess' belongings."

"Please do not speak nonsense. The first prince of the Largole Empire stepping foot into the Alain Kingdom without prior written notice could spark an international conflict."

"That's strange. The name Lukius Aidemoke should be on the list of baggage attendants."

Who the hell looks closely at the list of attendants?

I immediately wanted to check the list of names from immigration, but those documents were in my luggage back at the villa.

I want to keep that man away from the villa, but I don't have an excuse. I can't send him back to the empire because he already put his name on the list of baggage attendants and submitted a written notice.

Damn it, why won't you people in the Royal Administration of Foreign Affairs do your job right? I'm going to kick some asses when I get back.

"Lady Rosalite? You're Lady Rosalite, right?"

As I stood there, grinding my teeth while I thought of revenge, a bright and bubbly voice rang out from behind Prince Lukius.

The owner of the youthful voice, befitting her tender age of eighteen, came up to greet me, her wavy golden hair fluttering in the wind.

Oh my, what an honor to be greeted first. I need to show my respects.

"I appear to have been struck dumb by Your Imperial Highness' beauty, Princess Irini. Please forgive my discourtesy."

"No, no, it's fine! I understand if you didn't recognize me. Even in the imperial palace, I'm treated like a trivial princess, almost like a ghost! I am so pleased to make your acquaintance, as I heard you flipped the Largole Empire on its head while you were there!"

Uh...

This girl is a bit too bubbly.

I told the imperial princess she spoke Alainian very well as I accepted her enthusiastic handshake, and then I sidled up to the first Imperial Prince to compliment how well his sister had grown up.

I've never heard her name before, but it wouldn't hurt to get cozy with her if the first prince likes her.

"You must care for her very much if you volunteered to follow as her bellboy, Your Imperial Highness."

At my casual comment, the man cocked his head to the side and plopped one of the bags into my arms. "Huh? I've never met her before this."

"What...?"

"Ahaha! If I had known she was such an interesting child, I would have gone to see her long before."

Whaaat? Is this how sibling relationships are in the imperial palace? I know you have different mothers, but you've never seen your little sister in eighteen years?

I was truly shocked, and the two siblings seemed to find my expression entertaining. They linked arms like they had the best relationship in the world and told me how things actually were.

"My mother has aaabsolutely no money or power, so she lives out of sight as much as possible! People don't even know I'm a princess when I walk around the imperial palace!"

"Hahaha. That's right!" Prince Lukius said. "I didn't even know we had eight princesses."

"Your Highness, there are thirteen of us, not eight. I am not the last one."

"Ah, I see. But why are you calling me 'Your Highness?' Call me 'Big Brother.' You'll become a queen if things work out well. So, now is the opportune time to build on our relationship."

"Oh my, Big Brother. You really would use anyone and their mother if you deemed them beneficial to you."

"You are truly an entertaining child! How come I've never heard of you until now?"

Wow, yeah, okay. It's great to see you two getting along as siblings.

I turned to give the bag that Prince Lukius had forced on me to Aster when I felt a weird vibe from her.

Her eyes were boring into Princess Irini's face, and an undulating growl dripping with hostility escaped her throat as she positioned herself to draw her blade.

Oh my God, she's going to make a mess.

Just as the thought crossed my mind, Jack made his move.

He thwacked hard at the back of Aster's head, showering her with a bucket of swear words, and then whipped out his piano wire to tie her sword firmly inside its scabbard.

"Why did you do that, Aster?" I scolded her. "I told you to control your—"

"But the smell!"

Smell? What smell?

Confused, I asked Aster to tell me the details, and she informed me that there was some kind of chemical smell coming from the imperial princess.

"Isn't that just... the smell of her cosmetics?"

"It's probably makeup," Jack said.

"No! It isn't, little miss!"

My. I thought I'd never see the day you lost your temper with me, Aster.

Fascinated by her actions, I laughed indulgently and took her sword from her to give it to Jack. "Did you know that she tried to attack the duke the other day? I swear, she growls at anything these days, so keep her in check, Jack."

"This is why you bothered to bring me here?"

"That's correct."

"Well then. I suppose I have no choice."

I can't see his face because of the gas mask, but I can definitely tell he's excited.

Apparently thinking he had permission to hold Aster's leash, he popped a few kicks on her butt and took the bag from me before heading toward the carriage.

"Shall we go as well, then? You must be exhausted from your journey overseas. Allow me to show you somewhere you can rest."

Leading the imperial prince and princess to the VIP carriage, I edged into the seat next to Prince Lukius and whispered in his ear. I respectfully asked him what kind of garbage he was trying to pull under the pretense of being the luggage guy, and he laughed as he always did.

"Vacation," he remarked innocently.

"Cut the bullshit."

"You've become far more ill-mannered than before."

"This island belongs to the Alain Kingdom, and we have more people on our side, so why should I feel inferior?"

"Vacation and headhunting."

You're still going on about that...?

He commented that he would make me a countess if I betrayed my country. Unable to even laugh at him, I retorted that I would think about it if he made me an archduke before I moved my seat to sit next to the imperial princess.

"You must have suffered so much with someone like him as your older brother."

"No, not really," she replied. "I've never even met him until now."

You're right.

What she said was painfully true, but I didn't want to laugh at their inside joke, so I kept my mouth shut.

"..."

Now that I'm this close, she does kind of smell like disinfectant. Does she disinfect everything she wears because she's a germaphobe, too? If that's the case, then she and the Crown Prince are destined for each other...

Having met the imperial princess, I felt she was a good person, and my heart softened.

If these two younglings truly fall in love through this meeting... Hmm... only a terrible person would sabotage them.

She's a powerless princess, so if I pushed for a woman from our duchy to be taken in as a mistress, she wouldn't dare object. I'll think about this more after I see how her meeting with Theodore goes.

With that thought in mind, I chitchatted with the siblings as we headed to the royal villa.

Will this meeting go well?

Less than two hours after I resolved to bless their future marriage, my decision was deeply shaken.

This is bad! Our prince looks terrified.

It all happened exactly five minutes ago. Theodore the Smiling Face had finally woken up from his nap, dressed nicely, and agreed to have teatime with the rest of us. He then headed to the reception room, nervous and displeased at the unexpected sight of Prince Lukius.

I cajoled and comforted the Crown Prince, informing him that Prince Lukius was only on vacation, and not here to play games. I soothingly told him that all he had to do was spend some alone time with the imperial princess, then I opened the door. The sight of Prince Lukius, eating a bunch of grapes while stretched out luxuriously on a sofa, and a frozen stiff Princess Irini unfurled before our eyes.

Lukius was always like that, so I wasn't surprised. But there was something awfully strange going on with the imperial princess. She stared at Theodore as though she was seeing something unbelievable, then suddenly tramped toward us and fell to her knees at his feet.

She started weeping.

"Boohoohoohoo! He's so handsomeee!"

Sh-she's doing something that even I could never dare to do to Prince Marius...!

She bawled her eyes out, crying so much that the tears dripping from her eyes fell to the carpet and bled into each other wetly.

Even Prince Lukius froze in the middle of chewing the grape he had just popped into his mouth, taken aback by her actions. The Crown Prince, who had been terrified already, staggered backward.

"What are you doing, Your Royal Highness?" I said to the Crown Prince. "Help her up. She has traveled far from the empire just to meet you."

"B-but..."

"No buts! Hold out your hand."

You're the one who wanted this meeting.

I shoved him forward, and the Crown Prince discontentedly held out a hand toward Princess Irini. His entire body radiated horror at his situation, but he was still smiling. I had never been so relieved that his smile was a default setting.

Good boy, Your Highness. Magnificent, Theodore the Smiling Face. You are the model example of royalty.

"Hello... N-nice to meet you. My name is Theodore Alain."

Nice... to meet you?

Why does he sound like someone in a beginner foreign language textbook?

The way he stammered and stuttered as he awkwardly held out his hand was embarrassingly funny, but nobody laughed.

I actually wanted to give him a round of applause. He had tried his best. The way he did not run from the strange person in front of him and instead held out his hand to her was a beautiful sight to behold.

"Ack!"

The princess let out a weird half-scream of emotion, or God knows what, and the hand the Crown Prince barely had under control began trembling again.

You can't run away, Crown Prince. Do you understand? You can't run away!

"Are... are you all right? Your... hand..."

Hang in there, Theodore! You can do it!

I cheered him on inwardly, balling my hands into fists without even realizing it. *You're doing well. That's it. Get down on one knee, and... Yes! Grab it! Grab her hand!*

"Urk...!"

The imperial princess hesitantly reached for the Crown Prince's hand, then suddenly covered her mouth as she quivered from head to foot. Her face went pale in an instant.

SEVENTY

"I am very sorry."

What? Why? What are you sorry about? I knew it. Is he not as handsome as you thought up close? Falls short of your expectations, huh?

"I'm so happy I'm going to puke."

The imperial princess sprang to her feet and howled "Bathroom!" to one of her maidservants. The way she yanked her skirts up and stormed out of the room indicated she was about to hurl.

"Haaa..." When she was gone, the Crown Prince grabbed his head and swayed in place as though he had either relaxed or fallen into a state of panic.

I hastily supported him because he looked like he would fall over, and a royal maidservant handed me a handkerchief.

"Are you all right, Your Highness? Please keep it together. You haven't even introduced yourselves yet. There is still a long way to go."

"Y-yes, I... I know... that..."

Oh no. He's in shock.

He's grown up in the palace, so it makes sense that he would be stunned by someone as weird as her. Even I find her a bit alarming, and I've had years of experience with weird people.

"Here, Your Highness, have some water. Come on now, drink up while it's nice and cool. Take one sip at a time. Oh no, look at how much you're sweating."

I made the Crown Prince drink a cold glass of water so he could calm himself, and I diligently wiped away his sweat. Normally, he would've pushed me away, but right now, he was clinging to me like a rollercoaster restraint.

"Will you stay here the whole time?"

"Of course, Your Highness. I shall stay with you even after all this is over to make sure you arrive safely at the royal palace."

"Good. That's good, then."

The Crown Prince took a deep breath and quickly returned to his normal state. He stopped sweating and did not wish for me to help him stand anymore.

I guess he's made up his mind to put up with her for one day.

"Uh..."

Prince Lukius, who had been munching on grapes while Princess Irini went to puke, halfheartedly sat up and held out a hand to Theodore. Looking slightly awkward for being so taken aback earlier, he comforted the Crown Prince with a completely new attitude.

"I apologize for our princess' rudeness... Are you all right?"

"It is all right," Theodore replied. "I am sure she is just not used to this kind of situation, being as young as she is."

"I'm only here as a baggage attendant, so please treat me comfortably."

What a relief. It seems like we can continue the meeting.

Once the three of us had regained our cool, we were able to keep calm even after the imperial princess returned. She also appeared calmer than she had before and gazed openly at the Crown Prince while speaking as little as possible.

I know exactly how you feel because I feel the same way about the third Imperial Prince. But don't you think you're staring too much?

"Well then, I guess we've intruded on the young'uns long enough."

Oh? Prince Lukius, you have the mental capacity to say something so conventional?

I agreed with Prince Lukius that it would be best to leave the two to themselves and stood up from my seat.

I could feel a hand clutching at the skirt of my dress under the table. I didn't have to look to figure out it belonged to the Crown Prince.

"Hold on," he protested. "Didn't you say that you had something you would like to ask Princess Irini, Lady Rosalite?"

"Huh?"

"You know... you're both similar in age, and... so you had something to... ask."

Should I ignore him or not? When I thought about the haughty way he usually treated me, it was enough to make me want to leave him here ten times over. However, right now, he was grasping at me pitifully.

He seemed to be silently mouthing "please" over and over again.

Uhm... fine. I'll give in this time.

"Oh, right... I had something I wanted to ask."

The Crown Prince sighed in relief. "Oh good, you finally remembered."

With my eyes, I told Prince Lukius I was going to stay for a bit, and then I thought about what I should ask the imperial princess. Remembering what happened with Aster earlier, I asked her what makeup she used.

Surprised at my question, she flapped her arms frantically and thought hard for a moment. Then she slumped her shoulders in dejection and told me she didn't know.

Yeah, she probably isn't interested in that kind of stuff since her maidservants do everything for her. She would have been cute if she didn't barf at the sight of the Crown Prince... Her flappy arm thing just now was super cute and fitting for her age, too.

I still had a mind to sabotage their meeting, but honestly, it would be all good if they just had a baby, so my evaluation of the imperial princess was pretty high at the moment. *They'll probably pop out a baby soon since she likes him so much. She looks like she'll drag the Crown Prince into making one even if he vehemently refuses.*

Good, good. Very good.

They will probably have a cute, blond baby since they're both good-looking, too. Just looking at Theodore pisses me off to no end. But thinking about how I could influence his successor makes me happy. Once I nurture him to my liking, it'll be smooth sailing for our country!

Wait... is this why the duke is so soft on the Crown Prince?

My cheerful fantasy soured like milk in the hot sun at the thought of the Crown Prince, so I only stayed in my seat for another half hour. When the time was up, I stood and left the room after giving the Crown Prince some courage.

I was anxious about leaving him alone with her. However, he managed to stay in his seat until the end, and the couple even went for a walk in the garden afterward.

The window in the third-floor hallway had a fantastic view of the garden, so I took Aster and Jack with me to spy on the Crown Prince and the imperial princess. We crouched low and peered outside at the grounds with only our eyes visible.

"Is life fun when you live like that?" Prince Lukius asked.

"Yes, Your Imperial Highness."

"Really...?"

Hasn't he given up on his headhunting? Why is he following me around?

Though Prince Lukius had left the room before me, he had been waiting for the entire thirty minutes.

He said something about how being alone was boring, but how is playing with me entertaining when he's over thirty years old?

Then again... hanging out with younger people is pretty fun. Yeah. Hanging out with youngsters makes you feel more alive and energetic, like life is more vibrant. I guess it makes sense that he would follow me.

"Don't you have anything better to do, Your Highness? Why are you fooling around here? What about the fight for the throne?"

"I left my slow, idiot little brother in my place. And the little asshole Nerva is absorbed with some other matter these days, so it's not even fun to fight him."

Poor Prince Marius. I have a feeling I know what the fourth prince is absorbed with, but I shouldn't say anything. Aster may throw a fit.

"I would have been happier to see the third Imperial Prince if I was going to meet someone unexpected here."

"What? Are you one of Marius' fangirls, too?"

"Yes."

"Why...? There's no reason for someone from the kingdom to like him."

He's really grumbling so candidly now that he's on vacation.

Displeasure dripped from his voice, and he scowled hard with every facial muscle he could use. He didn't even have his eyepatch on, so I could see his severely scarred lid draped over his sunken eye socket. He looked like a scary pirate captain, scowling with that face while wearing casual clothes.

Not that he scares me or anything.

"Well, Prince Marius is like this and like thiiiiiiis!" Still crouching, I motioned with my hands to outline huge pecs and a thick booty.

Prince Lukius looked confused for a moment before carefully putting his own hands on his chest. "Are you trying to tell me he has a big chest and large buttocks?"

"Yes."

"That's the only reason you like him?"

"Yes."

"Are you insane?"

"No."

I was completely serious, and there were many fans of Prince Marius because of those reasons. *It's not just me and Luke. There are loads of people in this world who froth at the mouth for a glimpse of Prince Marius' sexy bod.*

When I told Prince Lukius so, he started squishing his own chest with a grim expression.

Stop that. You're making me feel sorry for you. Massaging your flat chest isn't going to make it any bigger.

"Give up, Your Highness. You have to be born with it."

"Wouldn't they get big if I worked out?"

"At your age, the only things that will get big when you work out are droopy muscles."

"You're extremely arrogant now that you're in your own territory."

"Try dragging me back to the empire if you are salty about it. I shall be meek and obedient then."

"No thanks. That doesn't sound any better."

I never realized it, but you're a genius at getting under my skin, too. How come you are Prince Marius' brother? In terms of odiousness, you're practically identical to my Crown Prince.

"Anyway, what is this?"

Oop! I knew he would be interested in Jack's gas mask.

Highly intrigued by the spyglass gas mask, Prince Lukius stretched his hands toward Jack's face, practically throwing a tantrum in order to try it on just once. Jack leaned away from him as far as he could, staring at me all the while.

Jack doesn't even want to let me use it, so he'd never give it to the first prince.

"Why are you trying to mess with his toy? Have some dignity."

"Don't be so surprised," Prince Lukius replied, "but I literally thought my wife had returned from the dead."

"If I was your wife, you wouldn't have a back from all the times I would have smacked it."

At my garbage retort to his garbage comment, Prince Lukius finally took his attention off Jack's gas mask and turned back to me. He asked me if I put the sailboat he had gifted me to good use.

When I told him that magnificent sailboat was currently playing the remarkable role of a tourist cruise ship along the Alain Kingdom coastline, he praised me for being a moneygrubbing leech.

This is nice. Spying on the Crown Prince and Princess Irini isn't half as boring when I get to chitchat with Prince Lukius.

I was thinking that the weather didn't look so good because of the ominous, rolling clouds, when a worried voice floated through the air behind us, calling for someone named Angela.

I turned my head and saw a woman wearing an imperial palace uniform, looking around in a slightly panicked sort of way.

"What is the matter?" Prince Lukius called out to her in a handsome, regal voice, but it didn't really help because he was still squatting with one hand on the window ledge to keep his balance.

The woman, however, did not seem astonished by his comical stance and bowed deeply before explaining her current plight. "I apologize for the inconvenience, Your Highness. I am one of Her Highness, Princess Irini's maidservants, and I cannot seem to find one of my workmates…"

"I certainly haven't seen you before."

Well, obviously... you've never seen Princess Irini before today, so it's obvious that you wouldn't know her maidservants.

Now that his curiosity was satiated, Prince Lukius told her she could go on her way. She bowed and apologized once more, and then continued to search for Angela.

"It looks like it's going to rain, Your Highness."

"Yes, it's windy, too."

"It was so bright and sunny earlier."

"That's how sea weather is."

"Shall we go and fetch the pair before the droplets start falling?"

"Yes. Otherwise, they might catch a cold."

You know how to worry about people, too!

I was impressed, but I didn't show it. Before I went to look for the lovey-dovey couple strolling in the garden, I called a servant to have some towels and hot bathwater ready.

The moment I found the Crown Prince to tell him the weather did not look promising, chance became certainty, and fat droplets of rain started streaming down.

Not long after, torrential rain began to pour on us, so we tossed away all dignity as we booked it back into the villa. Thanks to the orders I had given before I went out to search for the Crown Prince, we were able to get out of our wet clothes and immediately sink into nice, hot baths.

CHAPTER
SEVENTY-ONE

After we cleaned ourselves up, we went to dinner, and then each of us went our separate ways to enjoy some free time. The Crown Prince had warmed up considerably to Princess Irini despite being terrified of her in the beginning, so I gave her a few words of encouragement before leaving with Aster and Jack to play cards in my room.

The three of us scurried around the villa, looking for a blanket to spread out on the floor and making late-night snacks to munch on as we played. Prince Lukius had apparently noticed us preparing for a wild night because he showed up at my door with a bottle of expensive liquor and asked me to let him play.

I would have slammed the door in his face if he hadn't brought anything. But anyone who brings a good drink is a fabulous guest.

I warned him not to expect any princely treatment since Aster and Jack were my close guards, my hands and feet. Prince Lukius agreed to the condition and accepted a shot from Jack.

Upon realizing that our "wild night" literally only consisted of childish card games, Prince Lukius looked aghast, but then degenerated into rolling on the floor when he picked the Joker card during a game of Old Maid.

With a sudden frown, Aster sprang to her feet in the middle of shuffling the cards.

"...?"

"What is it, Aster?"

She closed her eyes and sniffed at the air. Even though we were still playing, she strode to the door to put her hand on the knob before turning to me. "I smell something burning, little miss."

"Burning?"

"Like the smell of burning meat."

Child... your sensitivity to the scent of food is remarkable.

I decided to take a look because burning meat was undeniably unfortunate, so I excused myself and followed Aster out of the room.

As I trotted down the hallway after her, she opened the door to a guest room not far from mine instead of the kitchen.

Upon opening the door, we were immediately engulfed by the unmistakable smell of something burning. Is there a fire?

The furniture looked pristine, and the only fire was burning in the fireplace.

It seemed kind of weird for a fire to be burning in an unoccupied room.

"This is..." Aster marched to the fireplace without hesitation and grabbed the poker. She began poking at something that looked quite large and lumpy.

It was large like a human body, to be exact, and it looked like a piece of meat that had shrunk in high heat.

"Is that a human body?"

"Yes, little miss."

It was a charred body.

"Aster."

"Yes, little miss."

"Crown Prince Theodore's safety is the top priority. Go let the head of his guard know."

We need to let them know and prepare to set sail when the storm recedes, even if it is at dawn.

Aster did not move an inch. When I scolded her for still being here, she argued that the premise of my order was wrong to begin with. "Your safety is my top priority. I cannot leave."

Do you really want to get into semantics right now? You uptight little knight!

I had never been able to wear down her stubbornness when it came to food and my safety, so I decided to find Jack first. I quickly extinguished the fireplace and hurried to my room.

When I arrived, I saw that Jack was looking a bit giddy, and I realized that the first prince must have forced him to drink. A powerful need to smack the shit out of Prince Lukius for incapacitating my guard in this urgent situation boiled inside me.

"Jack, can you run?"

"Yep, little miss. I only had... two drinks."

"We found a corpse. We will make the Crown Prince's safety our highest priority and set sail the minute the storm dies down."

Jack scrunched his eyes shut at my words and smacked his own cheeks a few times to clear his head. He replied that he would speak to the head of the royal guard and come back when they were ready to leave.

"You should also gather the imperial princess and your people, Prince Lukius. I am going to return to the scene of the crime and search for clues that could determine the killer."

"Wait," he replied.

Why? What now? I'm busy!

I staggered backward as Prince Lukius grabbed my skirt to heave himself to his feet. Even with Aster's help, I barely regained my balance.

He's over thirty and still acts like a child.

"The Crown Prince's safety is the highest priority? Does that mean I'm second?"

"Yes."

"But I'm Lukius Aidemoke."

"You came here as a baggage boy."

"My real job is being a prince, though."

It's like I'm talking to a wall. Why is he complaining about being second, anyway? At least I'm telling him that his safety comes before mine.

"As you know, Prince Lukius, human life is measured by importance."

"So, you're saying that my life is worth less than that of Theodore of the Alain Kingdom?"

"I did not say that. You are exaggerating, Your Highness."

"But that's what you meant."

"It isn't wrong to feel a bit more favorable toward my own Crown Prince in this dangerous situation."

So stop bothering me and go protect your own princess! I relayed my inner scream in the nicest way possible and hurried back to the room with the fireplace.

Aster followed silently behind, but I heard an extra set of footsteps.

"I thought I told you to go protect the imperial princess, Your Highness?"

"I have no reason or excuse to protect her," Prince Lukius said.

"Coming with me could be dangerous."

"That space next to you seems like the safest place in this villa."

"That's..."

Something I can't deny.

It was only an assumption, but the strongest person on this island was probably Aster. Not only that, but Jack would be back soon. He could beat even aura users into a pulp.

And I can use enough magic to protect myself, although that bit of information isn't widely known... Huh. I guess we're a pretty flawless combination.

"Fine. In return, you can't blame us if something happens to the imperial princess."

"I don't think so."

Ugh, I wish I could hit him. I wanted to pound Prince Lukius' obnoxious face in, but I clenched my fists and calmed my temper.

It'll be an international problem if I punch him. It'll be an international problem if I punch him.

"This island belongs to the Alain Kingdom," he said. "It's your country, so your country needs to take responsibility."

"Then the Roxburgs will take that responsibility. Let's not drag the entire country into this."

"Just the thought of the Roxburg dad and daughter combo working overtime at my house makes me very happy."

The hell! I thought you said you'd make me a countess! If you want to take an influential person away from her country, you at least need to give her some land that circulates a lot of money and a huge mansion in the capital!

I argued with Prince Lukius about going back on his word.

He slyly replied that the treatment between a plundered bigshot and one who comes to his country on her own would obviously differ. "So why don't you seek asylum? I'll give you a county that makes a lot of money and build you an enormous mansion within 109 yards of the main gates of the imperial palace."

"Never mind," I replied. "I'll just take the blame and kill myself."

"Can you not say such things? The person next to me looks like she's about to slaughter me."

Surprised at his words, I whirled around to see Aster next to the first Imperial Prince, glaring at him as though she would strangle him at any moment. *Calm down, Aster. I'm not going to die, so calm down.*

Even a blind man could have seen the hostility radiating from her, so I whacked her in the back as hard as I could and bowed low in apology to Prince Lukius. Then, I grabbed Aster's ear and dragged her all the way to the room with the fireplace.

Once inside, I told her to stand facing the wall to reflect on what she had done wrong. Aster glumly shuffled over to a corner of the room and put her forehead on the wall.

"It reeks in here," Prince Lukius muttered.

"That is why I told you to go and stay with the imperial princess, Your Highness."

"Being with a strange woman I don't even know is awkward."

"And being with a strange man I do not even know is awkward for me, Your Highness."

"I think we know each other quite well."

"I agree. It would have been better if we did not know each other."

As we lit a light and crouched down to observe the charred carcass, Prince Lukius finally said something useful.

"It looks like a woman."

"Does it?"

"See this? The hips are wide."

"As expected of someone who has fooled around with many women."

"Of course. I was married twice."

"Yeah, yeah, good for you." I answered him absentmindedly and poked at the corpse a little bit longer before getting up.

As I searched the room for any other clues or evidence, the first Imperial Prince asked me what I was doing.

"I think she died from a blow to the head, so I wondered if she was killed here."

"Her head?"

"Yes. Her skull is bashed in. Poke her with the fire iron."

"No, it's gross."

How did you look so closely at the hips, then?

I could not find any evidence of blood because the night was already dark, but under my feet, a part of the carpet was wet. I stood up to face the window, opened it, and looked down at the grounds outside.

I can't see anything in this darkness, but my assumption is probably correct. Anyway, the storm is getting worse. I wonder if a typhoon is coming.

"What are you doing over there?"

"Nothing, Your Highness. Shall we go back?"

"Already?"

Yeah, I found out everything I wanted to know, so I'm done playing detective.

The vase of fresh flowers placed in every single guest room was missing from this one. The entire villa had been refurbished specifically for this marriage meeting.

The killer must have struck the victim on the back of the head with the vase and tossed the broken pieces and the flowers out the window. That's why the carpet was wet even though the window wasn't open.

If the killer simply wanted to kill the victim, they would have left the body. They probably burned it, so it would be impossible to identify. That meant the murder wasn't spontaneous but planned in advance.

 SEVENTY-TWO

The victim might have been called into this room by someone she knew. It wasn't assigned to anyone or scheduled to be used today. The fireplace was also big and the chimney wide, so the room was very well ventilated. No one would have noticed the smell if not for Aster.

Whatever the case, this was a deliberate murder. *I don't give a shit about the motive as long as it's not some thrill-seeking maniac, so I'm just going to protect the Crown Prince and go home.*

I locked the windows just in case and went back to my room. There, I bundled up the playing cards and the blanket into my arms, and then took everything to the Crown Prince's room as Aster and Prince Lukius followed.

I'm going to stay in Theodore's room even if he tells me to fuck off. Jack and Aster will be with me, too.

"Your Royal Hiiighnesss! Your cutie, Rosalite Roxburg, is here!"

I should talk to him like I normally do so he doesn't freak out.

The Crown Prince might have been trembling in fear after hearing someone had been murdered, so I playfully let my presence be known and received permission to enter.

A royal maidservant opened the door for me. I marched in with my armful of stuff and began setting up my sleeping area near his bed. I flapped my blanket neatly onto the floor.

"What the hell are you doing?" Theodore demanded.

Took you long enough.

After I ordered the royal maidservant to bring me a duvet, I fluffed a pillow and got ready to lie down. "I'm making my bed, Your Royal Highness."

"Why?"

"I'm going to sleep here."

"Why?"

"I was worried you might not be able to sleep in a house with a dead body."

"Get out."

"Nooo!"

The Crown Prince almost retched at my mini tantrum, but then he saw Prince Lukius and calmed down. He seemed confused that the first Imperial Prince was also spreading out a blanket on the floor.

"What are you doing, Prince Lukius?"

"I thought I'd sleep here, too."

"...May I ask why?"

"I am scared to sleep alone."

Even the high and mighty Prince Lukius is human, after all. It's pouring and thundering outside with lightning crackling all over the place, and there's a goddamn killer who stuffed a person into a fucking fireplace and burned them to death roaming the villa. Of course, he's scared.

I can't sleep alone in this situation, either. I'm going to sleep sandwiched between Jack and Aster, holding each of their hands.

As I sat there, nodding my head in agreement, the Crown Prince suddenly stood up and put on an outer garment and a pair of gloves like he was going somewhere.

"Where are you going, Your Royal Highness?"

"I shall leave. You two can sleep together."

"Oh, no. That is inappropriate for a man and a woman."

"Are we not a man and a woman, Lady Rosalite?" Prince Lukius asked.

"It is completely different for us. It is not right to view the relationship between a ruler and a subject as such."

As though indelibly impressed by my words, Prince Lukius nodded. *I guess he's been through the same thing. Yeah, there's no "man and woman" between people who work together.*

"Get. Out."

"This is all for your safety, Your Royal Highness. Just bear with me for one night."

"Are you saying you would die for me?"

"If it comes to that, then yes."

I'd rather do another round of sixteen-year-old Rosalite than take on the responsibility of a dead Crown Prince on top of the responsibility of international problems.

I flung myself under the covers and Theodore stayed silent for a while, as though at a loss for words. When he spoke again, he asked me a ridiculous question.

"Are you actually in love with me?"

What the hell is this childish reaction?

The image of elementary school kids running around and chanting, "She loves you! She luuurrrves youuu!" bounced around in my head. But I knew that he would bicker more if I showed him how disgusted I was, so I tried to stay calm.

"Yes, Your Royal Highness. I love you very much, so go to bed. You won't grow up big and strong if you don't sleep well at night."

Good. It looks like he's finally going to shut up.

The man looked flabbergasted at my answer, then meekly took off his outer clothing and his gloves before climbing back into bed. I asked him if Aster and Jack could sleep with us since we were all here anyway, and Theodore shot back that he didn't know why I even asked when I did whatever I wanted anyway.

Didn't someone else say the same thing to me before…? Do I really act like that?

Well… not that it even matters.

I spread out some blankets for Aster, and when Jack came in to make his report, I had him sleep next to her and tucked him in.

We were all perfectly safe now. Jack ordered the servants to securely lock all the windows and doors of the villa and told them to travel in groups of at least two people, so hopefully they felt a bit safer, too.

When the storm passes, I'll wake everyone up even if it's in the middle of the night, and we'll go back to the Vienarre Harbor. We should all move together. We'll take Prince Lukius and Princess Irini back to the mainland with us and then make arrangements to get them to the empire safely.

We can send someone to gather our luggage at a later date. Man, I'll have a lot of work to do when I get home. I'll need to reschedule another marriage meeting with Princess Irini, and bitch at the Royal Administration of Foreign Affairs, and…

I ordered a maidservant to lower the lights, and I passed out while I thought about this and that.

Tap.

Tap, tap.

Someone shook me awake.

"Little miss! Wake up, little miss."

Huh? Did something happen...? Did something scary happen?

Hm? Something... scary? Sca...

"What is it?!"

I bolted upright when I remembered the corpse in the fireplace, and Jack hastily covered my mouth with his hand. Shushing me because everyone else was still asleep, he pointed a finger toward the window with a petrified look on his face.

"There's a weird noise coming from over there."

"A weird noise?"

Tap, tap, tap.

Yeah, that is a weird noise.

"Isn't it just the rain?"

"No, it's not, little miss."

"You sound confident about that."

"Because it can't be the sound of rain."

If it wasn't the rain, then it's probably the wind.

I told him so, yawning, but Jack would not accept it. He slipped his hands under my armpits to lift me up and pestered me to go and check.

"I'm telling you... you're just stressed out and overthinking things."

"Yeah, yeah, fine, little miss. Please just go check!"

It's the middle of the goddamn night!

Shoving a hand up the back of my pajama top, I scratched my back and quietly tiptoed to the window. I obviously could not see anything out of the ordinary outside because the room was on the second floor.

Tap, tap.

"There's nothing here."

"But there's still the weird noise, little miss."

"Yeah, but..."

I felt a slight quiver from Jack, who had wrapped his arms around one of mine. *Hm? Are his hands shaking?*

"Jack."

"Yes, little miss?"

"Are you scared?"

"You didn't know that until now?"

I mean, it's just that you've killed like a bajillion people, so I thought you didn't fear anything.

I asked him what he was so terrified of.

"Ghosts."

"Ghosts?"

"Ghosts."

"Right..."

This boy's real job is being an executioner who tortures and kills countless people in all sorts of ways in this world of magic and curses. In fact, he looks like he'd work with ghosts to kill people in a horror movie, but I guess he could be scared of them.

I tried my best to be empathetic to Jack's feelings and opened the window to look outside. I cocked my head so I could determine where the tapping noise was coming from and realized it was the front entrance area downstairs.

"I'll go check."

"Huh? Where are you going?"

"The front entrance."

It was cold, so I threw on a robe and left the room. Jack scurried after me, stuck to my arm like a piece of gum.

"Where do you think you're going all alone, little miss? Take me with you."

"I'm fine with going alone."

"I'm not."

You should be sleeping and snoring like Aster back there, even with the weird noises. However, it worries me that you're such a sensitive child.

I patted his arm to comfort him as I told him it was probably nothing, and then picked up a small lamp before heading downstairs.

The tapping noise became louder as we got closer to the front door.

Tap, tap!

"Be careful, little miss. Be careful. Seriously, be careful! I swear, you can't die and leave me alone!"

"You're hurting my ears."

Jack clung to me tightly as he shouted in my ear, and I became dizzy for a moment because of my temporary deafness. Squeezing my eyes shut and opening them again, I opened the door.

Bang!

Wow, the wind must be super strong.

The storm raged on outside like the beginning of an apocalypse, and streaks of lightning sliced through the sky as thunder rumbled and boomed. The door was ripped from my hands the moment I turned the knob because of the howling wind. It slammed into the adjacent wall as though it would smash it to pieces, and fierce sheets of rain drenched me to the bone.

I tried to find the source of the tapping noise that made Jack so anxious, even as the rain tried to drown me. But all I could see were the trees in the garden bending backward like they would break.

"A-agh! Aagghhh! Kyaaagghh!"

Holy shit!

Just as I was about to tell Jack there was nothing out here and we should head back now, a scream pierced my ear, deafening me again.

Wait, did you just yell "kyaaa," Jack?

"Did you see that, little miss?! A black thing! A black thing just went whoosh! Like whoosh! And whoosh!"

"There's nothing out there."

"There was, too!"

Stop that. You'll rip off my arm.

Jack anxiously stamped his feet. I felt like my arm might pop out of its socket, but I didn't have the strength to get him off me. I tried as hard as I could to find the black thing he had seen, while I let my body be shaken and rattled according to Jack's freak-outs, but I really could not see anything.

"I'm sorry I'm no help, Jack."

"Ughhh..."

You look like you're about to cry. Empathy is really important in a situation like this, though, isn't it?

CHAPTER SEVENTY-THREE

I wanted to scream and shriek with him about the black thing, but I couldn't because I didn't see it. The corners of Jack's eyes sparkled wetly in the dim light, so I squeezed his arm closer to my body, shut the door securely, and headed back upstairs.

"Let's hold hands while we sleep tonight. Wipe your tears now."

"I didn't cry."

"Okay, then."

If he says he didn't cry, then I guess he didn't.

Theodore was sleeping like a log when we returned to the room. I rolled Aster over to the side and made space for Jack to lie down next to me.

He brought a few towels from somewhere and rubbed my hair until it was dry. Then, he held my hand tightly as he curled up beside me.

I promised him repeatedly that I wouldn't let go of his hand, and I watched until his breathing evened out. He was sleeping peacefully before I closed my eyes.

It seemed as though the storm would go on for a little longer.

The next morning was dreary and didn't look like a morning at all.

Thick rainclouds darkened the sky outside, and the wind that had howled all night long still rattled the windows.

Prince Lukius and Theodore were nowhere to be seen despite our constant warning not to travel alone.

"Aster, where are the Crown Prince and Prince Lukius?" I asked.

"The Crown Prince still hasn't returned from his morning wash, and Prince Lukius has gone for a walk."

Who the fuck goes for a walk in this weather?

Nervous that the first prince might come to some harm while he traipsed around alone, I hastily washed up and dressed with Aster's help.

Princess Irini has no power in the imperial palace, so I can settle things on my own if she ends up dead, but Prince Lukius is different. The goddamn foundation of the House of Roxburg would be shaken to the core if he were hurt.

"Jack, tie my hair for me."

"What? Me?"

"Well, I can't ask Aster to do it, can I?"

Sitting on a chair and handing over a ribbon to Jack, who nodded in agreement, I told him to gather my hair in one hand and tie it tight. While he did my bidding, I lifted my foot to tie my shoelaces in turn.

It's such a hassle not having Lily or Violet here with me. I can't even call for other servants because they're in groups, acting as temporary security.

"You're really going out like this, little miss?"

"I'm sure the others will understand, since we're in the middle of an emergency."

"Nah, it's not that…"

Because there was no one to help me get dressed, I wore a pair of breeches and a dress shirt. *I'm sure they will accept my excuse that I wanted to be dressed comfortably in case something happened. But it's true that it isn't appropriate to be dressed like this in front of both royal and imperial palace members.*

"I do have an extra dress, so I could dress properly if you helped me put it on, Jack. Starting with my underskirts."

"No thanks. Let's just go, little miss. How you live your life isn't my business."

Why are you talking about life over an outfit?

After admonishing Jack about how exaggerating was a bad habit, I went to find the servants patrolling their predetermined areas of the villa in groups, and then had them relay a message for the others to come and have breakfast. After that, I went to find Prince Lukius. Apparently, my detective act yesterday seemed like fun to him, so he was speaking with servants to figure out the identity of the burnt corpse.

"Did you find out anything, Your Highness?"

"Not at all."

"Then could you please stop giving me heart attacks and just sit tight until you go home?"

"I don't know what to do with myself, seeing the unmatched lady of the Roxburg duchy worrying for me so."

"I would worry even if I were not a Roxburg, Your Highness. Besides, yesterday you said we were not strangers, did you not?"

Prince Lukius raised an eyebrow in surprise but followed obediently to the dining hall. *It's a relief that he at least pretends to listen when I tell him something.*

Not even fifteen seconds later, he pulled at my ponytail, saying, "Ding-dong!"

"Will you grow up, Your Highness?!"

"Your future husband must worry his poor heart because of you."

Why is he talking about Glen all of a sudden?

I huffed angrily, thinking he was just saying that because he had no excuse for teasing me, but Jack tapped me on the shoulder and shook his head.

"His Imperial Highness is right, little miss. You need to be good to Lord Glen."

What the hell? What did I do?!

Prince Lukius and Jack gave each other a look and a nod, as though they had shared some kind of message, and then they glared at me like I was a dirty sinner before they went on their way.

"Christ, no one is on my side, huh?" I muttered darkly. Aster stepped up and told me she did not understand what they were talking about either, but it wasn't really comforting.

What good is Aster taking my side? They all make me out to be the weirdo anyway.

When I arrived at the dining hall, I saw that Princess Irini was already there. I presented her with a seat right next to where the Crown Prince would sit, and I asked how her night was.

"You must not have slept well last night, Princess Irini. Your face looks a little unbalanced."

"Thank you for the concern, but I am fine."

The imperial princess told me she had been scared of the storm outside but was okay because her maidservants were with her. I felt a bit more relieved at her words.

Hm? Hang on, why didn't I bring Princess Irini to come and sleep with us? If I thought about her safety...

Oh yeah, I didn't think to do so because the Crown Prince might've really left the room if more people came to spend the night there. Thank God, nothing happened to her last night, though.

"May I ask where Crown Prince Theodore might be...?" she asked.

"Oh, that clean freak."

He's probably scrubbing at his body like he's cursing all the filth in this world.

I caught myself before I said the words out loud, and I rephrased my thoughts so I wouldn't crush the princess' fantasy about him. It would've been a pain in the ass to deal with the two if they blamed me for the prospective marriage not working out.

"The Crown Prince finds the utmost importance in cleanliness, so his bath hours are long. And I am sure he is taking longer than usual because he needs to stand before the woman he wishes to impress."

"Oh my!"

Child, what are you thinking? Why is your face turning red?

Yeah, we're stuck on this island anyway. Let's make something happen. They say that people's need to reproduce increases when their lives are threatened. If you get knocked up with a successor, you'll be tomorrow's Crown Princess of the Alain Kingdom. Good luck, Princess Irini!

"What are you all talking about so jovially without me?"

Oh, look! It's the devil! The devil!

The man who had spent all morning washing himself finally appeared while the imperial princess and I giggled and tittered.

The Crown Prince gave off a faint floral scent, like he wanted to show off that he had put in effort before meeting his marriage prospect. His face became unreadable as he looked me up and down.

"...What is with your getup?"

"We are in the midst of an emergency. I hope you will graciously understand my wish to dress comfortably in these circumstances, Your Royal Highness."

"Did your guard with the strange mask tell you?"

Tell me what?

I tilted my head to the side, as I had no clue what he was talking about. Theodore went around the long way of the table to avoid me, like he was avoiding something gross. He took his seat next to Princess Irini, huffing and snorting like he was scandalized.

Well, he's always been a weirdo, so I'll just let this slide, but... why does he keep sneaking glances at me like that? It's unpleasant.

"So," he said. "When can we return to the mainland?"

"I do not know, Your Royal Highness."

"And what have you been doing if not figuring that out?"

"I am not a weather tower that can predict when the typhoon will end."

It's true that it's my fault I didn't ask the ship's crew, who were staying in the servant quarters. But if you keep bitching like that, I'm not going to tell you!

As I cheekily ate the smoked ham laid out in front of us, the prince balled his fists.

The hell? You wanna punch me? Punch me, then! Forget our titles, let's have a showdown!

"I've already looked into it," Prince Lukius interjected. "We should be able to set sail tonight."

"As expected of the first Imperial Prince Lukius," Theodore replied. "You are truly in a different league, far out of reach from a certain duchy member I know."

"I am deeply moved by how you take the initiative in place of your servants, Your Imperial Highness. If only a certain Crown Prince would learn from your greatness."

"What do you mean, 'a certain Crown Prince'? Are you talking about the one living in Alain, Lady Rosalite?"

"There are many crown princes in the commonwealth, Your Royal Highness. Perhaps a certain Crown Prince is bristling because he feels guilty about something?"

"And perhaps a certain heiress to a duchy is a nagging, slow-witted person who doesn't even know when she is being mocked."

"Ugh, I don't know who she is, but I pity her for having a ruler who only speaks ill of her behind her back."

"She always tries to dance on the ruler's head, so what reason do you have to pity her?"

"Well, maybe the top of his head is a good place to dance!"

"Don't think for a moment that I am as generous as His Majesty the King!"

What are you going to do if you're so petty, then? Are you going to throw me in a prison cell for mutiny?!

The Crown Prince Theodore and I slammed our fists on the table and sprang to our feet in the middle of breakfast.

The imperial princess surreptitiously grabbed Theodore's sleeve and placed a hand on my shoulder to intervene.

"It is an honor to see the infamous arguments between the two of you with my own eyes, but please calm yourselves."

"H-he's right. Lady Rosalite, Crown Prince Theodore. We shall be able to leave the island tonight, so please do not fight," Princess Irini pleaded.

Just know that I'm going to keep my temper because I don't want to embarrass myself in front of the people of the empire!

As I "hmph"-ed and turned my head away from the Crown Prince, he fumed and stomped off.

When I saw his half-finished breakfast, I couldn't help but nag, no matter how hard I tried not to. "Where do you think you are going without finishing your breakfast?!"

"How am I supposed to force food down my throat in this situation? I do not have nerves of steel like the lady of the Roxburg duchy!"

"You won't get smarter if you skip breakfast!"

Oooh! Just look at that young'un stomping away without eating!

The Crown Prince left, leaving more than half of his food untouched, so I packed the leftovers and called for a group of maidservants to take it to the Crown Prince.

Princess Irini graciously said that she would go with them, so I decided to leave the Crown Prince to her. Stuffing the rest of my food in my face, I washed everything down with a glass of cold water.

"Would I get to see such entertainment every time I visit the Alain palace?"

"How is this entertaining? It is not fun one bit, Your Imperial Highness."

"Oh, yes, it is. I would have laughed my ass off if no one were watching."

"You have quite a low standard for comedy."

"I've led a life devoid of entertainment, you see."

Why? The stories I hear about the imperial palace are as entertaining as crazy soap operas.

I never mentioned them directly because it would be bad manners to talk about such spectacular incidents. In one infamous story, Prince Lukius' mother suffered so much from postpartum depression that she bashed in her firstborn's right eye not long after he was born.

What would be so entertaining about my country when people are socially ostracized and executed like flies on the daily in yours? From the first moment you open your eyes in the morning, you probably wonder if anything happened last night.

SEVENTY-FOUR

"By the way, Your Highness."

Since we were alone in the dining hall, I decided to ask something I had been wondering about. "Why is the imperial princess acting all alone?"

"How would I know?"

"What about her maidservants that were with her all night long?"

"I'm not close with that sibling of mine."

"Why did you come here?"

"I'm here as a baggage attendant, remember?"

"Because you were bored?"

"Because I was bored."

Horseshit.

Unable to actually say that out loud, I pursed my lips and chose my next words carefully. *Looking after the Crown Prince would probably be a bajillion times better than serving this prick.*

Long live Prince Theodore, hip-hip hooray!

"I do not know what you are scheming, Your Highness, but if it is anything that goes against the national interest of the Alain Kingdom, I will be on you like a rabid jackal."

"Rest easy. I'm not going to lay a hand on your kingdom yet."

"Yet?"

"Yet."

You expect me to believe that?

The way Prince Lukius acts make me think that living a long life will be vexing. Yeah, I'm going to kill myself when I figure out Rion's issue. I've done it a few times, so it isn't even hard for me anymore. What happens to the Alain Kingdom or the Roxburgs isn't my business once I'm dead.

As I sat there praying that Asterion would hurry up and grow to have a magnificent wish that I could fulfill and die for, a familiar scream reached my ears.

A male voice went "kyaaa" the same way it did at dawn today.

"Little miss! Little miss! Little miss! Little miss!"

Now what?

I was about to scold the man, who knew his manners better than Aster, but when he opened the door and barged in, I was at a loss for words. He and Aster were tightly hand in hand.

Why are they holding hands in such a friendly way?

"Little miss! We saw it!"

"Saw what?"

"That black thing from last night!"

Aster nodded her head vigorously.

Uh... I'm asking just in case, but...

"Aster."

"Yes, little miss?"

"Are you scared of ghosts, too?"

"Yes, little miss!"

I see...

What the hell kind of childhood did you Brown siblings have?

"Would you like to come with us, Your Highness? You are probably bored anyway."

Deeming it prudent to inspect what the two were freaking out over, I held out a hand to Prince Lukius and invited him to join me.

He pouted and primly crossed his arms. "You speak to me as if I'm a bored playboy with too much time on my hands."

"Are you not?"

"I am, actually."

His expression brightened as though he had never been pouting. Prince Lukius grabbed the hand I was holding out and ran to where Jack and Aster said they found the ghost.

He must be really, really bored.

"Over there, little miss, over there!"

Jack led us to a room in a long hallway that led to the central garden.

The door of the room had been barricaded with a table, a couch, a large vase, and a pile of different furniture. In a panic, they had shut the door upon hearing a strange thudding noise from inside, blocking it with furniture in hopes that the "thing" couldn't come out. They came running to find me at once, but...

I couldn't understand why they had been in this part of the villa during breakfast time in the first place, so I asked them for a reason. The two glanced shiftily at each other and tattled at once.

"That asshole threw my chuck roast slices on the floor and ran away, little miss!"

"Well, Aster eats with her face buried in the goddamn plate like she's been starved for three days! It's disgusting and made me wanna puke. Please teach her some manners, little miss!"

"You shouldn't throw food on the floor, Jack."

Especially meat, it's Aster's favorite food.

I flicked Jack's forehead and then told Aster I would make her take table-etiquette classes when she wasn't scheduled to be my guard.

As Aster and Jack alternated between laughing at each other and sulking, I told them to clear the way to the door. They lifted the heavy furniture out of the way with ease.

"I thought they were just some funny kids," Prince Lukius remarked, "but it turns out they're quite brawny."

"Ahem-hem! They are not just strong, Your Highness. They are also extremely competent guards."

"Well, I already knew that about one of them since I saw her with my own eyes, but..." Prince Lukius told me he thought Jack was a Roxburg bureaucrat because he was so scrawny, which greatly shocked Jack.

You should've eaten more than just bits of greens... I'm going to buy a bunch of meat when I return home and force him to eat some.

"Stand back. I'll take a look inside."

I planned to go in and check it out by myself, but Prince Lukius followed me inside. When we—the two people who had fearlessly taken the lead in this matter—disappeared into the room, Jack and Aster seemed to think their protectors were gone. So, they hastily followed us inside, asking us to wait up.

Why are you guys even coming inside when you're trembling like leaves?

"Do you see anything, little miss?"

"Little miss! On your left! Your left! Next to the partition... Aaagghhh!"

Wondering what the freakout was about, I turned to see that large shadows had been cast by the lightning flashes outside.

It was strange that Aster would scream at a few shadows, but I also felt there was something off about them. *The shadows are shaped like humans—meaning us—and there are one, two, three, four, five...?*

That's one more than the number of people here right now.

"Aaaggghhh! Uwaaahhh!"

"Kyaaa! Kya! Kiyaaagghh!"

"Will you two be quiet?!" I snapped, walking forward, as I recalled how the shadows had been cast upon the wall.

Let's see... the lightning came from over there, so the light would hit somewhere around here, which means the other human shape would be...

Thump. Thump.

Ah, here it is.

A small object squirmed around under an ornamental table, so I bent over and shoved my arm deep under it. Jack and Aster began screaming again.

Why does this remind me of so long ago, when I used to catch cockroaches in the house because my family were too afraid...?

"What is it?"

Jack and Aster covered their ears and screamed with their eyes shut. The only person who showed any proper reaction to the object dangling from my hand was Prince Lukius.

Well, uh... this... is... How should I explain it...?

"It's the... uh... Automated Return System-Enhanced Rosalite Roxburg Mach II..."

"The automated... what?

"The Automated Return System-Enhanced Rosalite Roxburg Mach II, Your Highness."

So, this is what that "black thing" was last night, huh?

I squeezed the water from the doll, which was soaked from the rain, and shook it out, then I brushed its hair back. Now it didn't look like a piece of seaweed that had been fished from the bottom of the sea, and we could see its pretty face.

Theodore must have forgotten to pack the doll when he came to the island. It's designed to automatically find him wherever he is, so it probably climbed the royal palace walls and crossed the ocean to get here.

No doubt, the doll tapped at the windows and doors to be let in since it couldn't open anything on its own. I'd had everything securely locked up... and when I opened the front door last night, Jack must have seen it dash in and freaked out.

...This doll is fucking amazing. It even crossed the ocean on its own!

"That doll looks a lot like you."

"Like I said, it is the Rosalite Roxburg Mach II, Your Highness."

I felt proud of the doll for coming all this way and hoped it would continue to work hard. I placed my hand where the mana crystal was and recharged it.

Prince Lukius looked back and forth between me and the doll. "I thought you only sold pastries, but you sell dolls, too?"

"No, Your Highness."

It's been ages since I quit the pastry business! Why are you talking about it now?

I had wanted to keep the business afloat, but there were those who found fault at every turn. Supposedly, the business instigated gambling and spotlighted the wealth gap because rich people threw away the pastries and only collected the trading cards. On top of it all, a whistle-blower exposed that I was committing fraud with the probability of the cards, so the king himself made me shut down the business.

I don't know who the whistle-blower is, but they're dead when I get my hands on them.

"The story about this doll is a long one, but if I summarize..."

"If you summarize?"

"Crown Prince Theodore sent me bread crusts as a wedding gift, and it made me very angry. So, I sent him the Rosalite Roxburg Mach II as a return gift so he would think about me while he slept and worked for the rest of his life."

"Poor man..."

And if you keep being annoying, too, I'm going to send you a Mach III.

While I was secretly making that resolve, Mach II finished charging and tried to wriggle out of my arms.

Jack and Aster were still covering their ears with their eyes squeezed shut, so I told them that it wasn't a ghost and showed them the doll. At the sight of it, they finally relaxed and took it from me.

"Oh, what? It was the doll this whole time?"

"But little miss ..."

"But what?" I asked. "There's no problem now that we know it isn't a ghost."

Aster replied that something was wrong and pulled at the Mach II's hair. She held up a black wad of something so that I could see it.

"This hair. It isn't your hair color, little miss."

"..."

"..."

"..."

No wonder the doll reminded me of a piece of seaweed earlier...

I looked down at the hand I had used to brush the tangles out of its hair and saw strands of black snarled around my fingers.

"And little miss, that table you found it under isn't placed up against a wall, so what was the doll bumping into?"

R-right... w-what was it hitting...?

I stared at my hand and then at the table, carefully getting onto my hands and knees so I could peek under it. I couldn't see anything because it was dark, but the smell of water and a foul, fishy stench assaulted my nostrils.

Crack!

Lightning followed a rumble of thunder, and an earsplitting crack, which sounded like lightning, tore the ground apart.

Its brilliant flare lit the room for a moment, and I could clearly see what was under the table...

Eyeballs.

My eyes locked with those of a woman.

Her wide, unseeing eyes bore into mine as her wet, plastered hair snaked around her face and back.

Her neck had been twisted backward.

The bone that stuck out from her throat glistened palely, and her entire body was bizarrely bent.

"Kyaaagghhh!"

I screamed with every last bit of air I could muster into my lungs and bolted upright into Aster's arms.

CHAPTER
SEVENTY-FIVE

Let's go home. Right now. We have to go home right now!

After waking the ship's crew by shouting that we had to set sail even if the ship flipped over in the middle of the ocean, I set Rosalite Roxburg Mach II onto the floor and followed it to find the Crown Prince.

I don't care about ghosts, but I'm not about to stay another second in this villa with a serial killer.

The things that had happened yesterday couldn't be helped, but another murder despite the assigning of groups meant the victim knew the killer. There was a high chance the killer looked harmless on the outside because they had been able to lure a woman away when everyone was so on edge. The killer could be someone I knew as well.

I don't care if Sadako or Marbas exist in this world, but Damien and serial killers freak me out. They look so innocent, but they turn right the fuck around and chase you with knives. That's a double attack of betrayal on both the mind and body!

As I plugged my ears and dashed to find His Highness, I thought I heard Prince Lukius laughing raucously behind me, but screw that. I wanted to pack up the Crown Prince and go home.

"Is he in there?!"

"Wait, Lady Roxburg! You must not enter at this moment!"

When I saw the Mach II bump its head on the door of a room two maidservants were guarding, I ran like the wind.

The maidservants on lookout formed a defense barrier to block my path, but I feinted left, then whirled to the right to sidestep them, and barged right in.

The dramatic scene inside the room unfolded before my eyes.

"…!"

"Mmph!"

Crown Prince Theodore lay on the wide bed, and Princess Irini's body was entangled with his. Judging by the way the Crown Prince's arms were tied tightly to the bedposts while the princess straddled him and muffled his mouth, it seemed she was in the middle of doing some pretty kinky stuff. The Crown Prince squirmed around, apparently impatient, and his wide eyes glared fiercely at me.

"Oh, uh… well, I, uh…"

…came in at a bad time, huh…? Yeah… I did, didn't I…?

I remembered all the incidents that had happened when I burst through doors unannounced, so I slowly turned my head away and walked backward.

I was thinking I should roam the halls for a couple of hours before returning, when Aster dashed toward the room.

"I see you're finally showing your true colors?!"

What...?

Aster snatched the sword Jack had confiscated and held it like a club while she dashed into the room. Theodore's face immediately brightened, and the imperial princess leaped away from the bed.

What the hell is going on? Can someone please explain?!

"Little miss! It's magic!"

Whaaat? It's what now?

"Lady Roxburg! Are your eyes mere decorations?!"

If Aster had been the only one to speak, I would have thought she was just hounding random people again, but the Crown Prince rebuked me as well, so I gathered my wits.

Magic? Eyes for decoration? Is this visual manipulation, then? Wait, "manipulation"? That means...

To confirm my suspicions, I gave myself a light smack on the face, which instantly cleared my vision. My eyes registered an uncanny sight, and I sensed a repulsive flow of mana.

If what I'm seeing is the truth, that means that I've been chatting and tittering amicably with someone wearing that thing.

"Aster, the face!"

"I know, little miss!"

The moment the attack order fell from my lips, Aster leaped toward the imperial princess, whacked her down with the sword still tightly bound in its scabbard, and reached out her hand to the princess' face.

When Aster yanked away her arm, the princess' skin astonishingly peeled away and revealed an unknown woman.

"Ugh! A little longer, and I would have had it!"

Had what? Kinky time with the Crown Prince?!

"I even bloodied my hands so I could meet Prince Theodore!"

She really wanted to jump him, then! Damn, I messed things up... Wait, no, I didn't!

I'm sorry, Your Highness! I thought for a second, you know, she's some chick from God-knows-where, but I mean... I thought if she got pregnant with a successor... it wouldn't be all that bad. Only for a second, though! Just one second, I swear!

"Eww! The hell is that, little miss? Face skin?"

I see. That was probably what Aster was talking about when she met the princess for the first time and said she smelled bad.

Considering I was able to dispel the dark magic with a single slap to the cheek, she couldn't perform high-level mental manipulation. However, she was able to create an illusion using the facial skin of someone she wanted to mimic, so it appeared she had killed the imperial princess and chemically treated the skinned face.

Oh yeah, I noticed her face was crooked this morning. But even then, it hadn't felt like anything was off.

Now that I've been through it, this mental manipulation thing seems really useful.

"It is as I thought."

And why are you butting in, Prince Lukius? Get back before you hurt yourself. I told you; I won't have my family become ruined because of you.

"The women who were murdered last night and today were the eighth princess' direct maidservants, were they not?" he asked. "This woman did away with them so her true identity would not be revealed."

"I thought you said your detective play did not bear any fruit."

"Yes, it did not... Until we discovered the second woman."

"What about the second woman?"

"Have you forgotten?" Prince Lukius said. "She was the eight princess' maidservant searching for someone named Angela."

"You have quite a knack for recalling the faces of women."

"I shall take that as a compliment."

Honestly, I didn't even make that connection because I was too busy running in shock. If that grotesque corpse with the twisted neck was indeed the maid from yesterday, then one could conclude that the burnt corpse was Angela.

"I apologize for the trouble caused because I did not realize my real sister was dead. Now, if you could subdue the culprit and hand her over, I shall handle the matter according to imperial law and—"

"Kill her, Aster!"

Don't be stupid. You think I don't realize that if I hand her over, you'll use her for some other sly tricks? For a moment, even I thought she might be useful in the right hands, so you'd probably suck her dry for all she's worth in a far more ingenious manner.

"That was harsh. I gave you Lem Baht, did I not?"

"Would the child truly have arrived at my place without a scratch if you had still needed her, Your Highness? Please do not give yourself too much credit."

"Regardless, are you not using the hand-me-down quite well, even if I do not need her any longer?"

"Yes, she is doing good work in our printing room."

"Printing room? Why on earth is she being used in a printing room...?"

As Prince Lukius' voice trailed off, Aster subdued the unidentified woman and broke her neck in an instant.

After the woman's head lolled onto her chest, Aster checked once more that she had stopped breathing and reported that she had fulfilled my orders.

"I told you she smelled weird!" she shouted angrily. Her face crumpled, and tears welled in her eyes. Apparently feeling extremely vilified that I hadn't believed her, Aster squatted down in front of me and bawled.

I stopped arguing with Prince Lukius and patted her back. "I'm sorry, I just thought you were giving into your bad habit..."

"But I told you! I told you right from the start!"

"Yes, yes, you did. I'm sorry, it's all my fault."

As I sat there, hugging Aster, Prince Lukius seemed to lose interest in squabbling with me and left the room, saying that we should make haste to the mainland.

Once Aster's tears subsided into hiccups, we stood up to leave the island as well.

A voice we had all completely forgotten about rang out behind us. "Hey."

When I turned my head, I saw that the Crown Prince was still tied to the bedposts.

"Untie me before you leave."

"Do you not have the strength to untie yourself, Your Royal Highness?"

"Yes, I am so incredibly weak I fear I do not have the strength even to meet the marriage prospect the Roxburgs have prearranged for me."

"Ah, you are perfect in every other manner, so you do not need something as trivial as strength."

I urged Jack to quickly untie the Crown Prince. Then, I beseeched the Crown Prince to consider Princess Natalie of the Principality of Nimernia as a potential match and hastened our preparations to return home.

The wind was still howling, but the weather was calmer than this morning.

Aboard the ship, on the way back to the mainland, I regretted that I had the mental manipulation mage killed. I did it because I didn't want the first Imperial Prince to have her, but perhaps it would've been more prudent if I had made her spill who was behind it.

I didn't think there was anyone behind her actions, but it was a necessary step I should have taken to reassure the Crown Prince.

A woman had killed the poor imperial princess and taken her face skin, bloodied her hands, and risked her life to have a little kinky time in bed with him. On top of that, she had duped everyone into thinking she was his marriage prospect. *Prince Theodore must be terrified.*

I wouldn't have blamed him if he said he would never meet another woman. In fact, the Crown Prince told me not to mention anything about marriage the moment his feet touched Vienarre Harbor.

I'm so going to get an earful from the duke.

Preparing myself for the worst, I headed home. As expected, the duke chewed me out endlessly while I kneeled on his office floor and wrote ten apology letters.

Once the duke examined my letters, filled from page to page, I barged into the Royal Administration of Foreign Affairs and flipped some tables. Then, I sent a list of the people who had let the "baggage boy" Lukius Aidemoke enter our country to His Majesty the King, suggesting he cut their wages.

A short while after, I received the news that their wages would be cut for a year, along with a message that the mother of the fourth Imperial Prince Nerva Tianus Largole's mother, Nicole Tianus, had passed.

I'd been wondering why that asshole Lukius came all the way to the Alain Kingdom. *I see now that he visited as an excuse not to be blamed for this.*

I clicked my tongue at the thought of another bloodbath in the empire, then I sent a letter to the fourth prince with my condolences for his mother's death and a scroll with a written "Congratulations!" to the first prince.

About a month later, when I had forgotten I even sent out those letters, the first Imperial Prince sent a letter to the heiress of the House of Roxburg. In the message, he said that he had no idea what I was talking about, and enclosed was a silver spoon.

He must have poisoned her. Seriously, what an evil bastard.

CHAPTER
SEVENTY-SIX

Sometime after Asterion's birthday, Fraude—who was temporarily staying at our house to aid Glen—screamed and ran back to the Veloce territory.

To be honest, he had come to my office day after day ever since I had returned from the island, begging me to send him back because he absolutely could not remain under the same roof as someone "as shady as a snake." Unfortunately, I couldn't let him leave without finding a replacement first. Glen needed someone to work for him, and I made that clear to him. That's why things ended up like this.

Did Fraude really have a good reason to ditch things without going through the proper procedures? And who the heck is the snake?

I was in the middle of writing up an urgent document, thinking that I'd have Philip take Fraude's place, when Violet announced Rion's arrival.

For some reason, Violet was even more excited than I was when Rion stepped inside, and she immediately rushed to the side room to prepare tea and snacks.

Uh, Violet... I didn't tell you to prepare anything...

"I am here for today's worth."

Yeah, sure.

While I continued to scribble away, Rion hugged me from behind, careful not to disturb my work. He rubbed his face on me, buried his nose in my hair, made weird panting noises, and played with my body until he was satisfied. Then he sat on my desk and crossed his legs.

"Mind your manners, Rion."

"You will forgive me anyway."

"Keep acting like that, and you'll be in big trouble one day."

"Aww, pwease."

At my slightly angry tone, Rion hastily jumped off my desk and linked his arm with mine.

I knew he did it so I wouldn't scold him, but... honestly, it was adorable. I couldn't help but think he was endearing, even though I knew he was being crafty. *I understand why emperors of the olden days ruined their empires for their concubines and whatnot. Like, who cares if Pao Shih wants two hundred yards of silk to be shredded daily if she's adorable?*

I let out a soft laugh as I continued writing. "Why are you here today?" I asked.

Rion watched my mood for a moment before removing his arm and stepping back. "I have yet to receive a birthday present from you."

"Yes. You asked me to wait until you made your decision."

"And I have, today."

All right, so what do you want?

When I urged Rion to tell me what he wanted, he cleared his throat and pointed at the display cabinet behind me.

In it was my May Bridal Edition Montecarlo Luxury Fountain Pen collection in every color. A prominent fountain pen craftsman had made them to celebrate his youngest daughter getting married. *Surely Rion isn't asking for that, is he?*

"Do you mean the golden squid statue that was made to commemorate my return from the empire?"

"No."

"I see, then you mean the Roxburg employee files. Is there someone you have in mind?"

"The May Bridal Edition Montecarlo Luxury Fountain Pen."

This punk has zero interest in stationery, but he knows the name of my precious pens?

"W-which color... do you want...?"

"The set."

Hey! I had to stand in line to get these myself!

My heart dropped to the floor when Rion asked for the pens I had acquired by spending my precious time standing outside the store all night long. I hadn't even used them properly yet because I was scared the nibs would wear down. Still, I couldn't show how I truly felt.

I've built up a certain image for myself, so I can't get stingy over some fountain pens.

"M-my dearest Rion. Your trainer praised you and said you'd be on Aster's level in a few years, yes? How about a nice sword that's perfectly balanced for your grip? I can even have it magically processed afterward if I ask Sir Sage."

"May Bridal Edition."

"If you don't want a sword, then what about a nice ring for your pretty hands? Luke told me he imported a huge diamond from the empire, so if we make a ring with that—"

"The whole set."

Did he plug his ears before he came here?

As I sat there racking my brain to come up with a different item to pique Rion's interest, my darling brother completely changed his expression. His head drooped, and his eyes filled with tears.

"You said... you said you would give me anything I wanted. That's why I plucked up the courage to ask..."

"Well, I mean, Rion—"

"I... can't have it...?"

He lifted his head slowly, his eyes red-rimmed. His shoulders had slumped forward slightly. *I guess he really just took me at my word... Does he want those pens that badly?*

I did say I'd give him anything he wanted, and how am I supposed to fulfill his wish later if I'm so stingy with a few pens...?

"I apologize for my impudence. I shall consider a different pres—"

"No! I'll give them to you! It's all right! They're yours!"

What if this pen set is his actual wish?

I hastily shouted that I would give him the set, and Rion's tears magically disappeared as he beamed.

This boy is experiencing some severe emotional ups and downs compared to the Rions before him. Do I need to bring in a therapist?

Even though I had yelled so confidently, I couldn't hide my trembling hands. Barely able to calm my pounding heart, I opened the cabinet and brought out the pristine fountain pen set without a speck of dust on it.

As I placed the set back into its box, looking dreadfully sorry to see them go, Rion excitedly bragged to Violet.

This was the first time I ever managed to buy these in my twenty-two lives...

"Violet! Look at this! My sister is gifting me the May Bridal Edition Montecarlo Fountain Pen Set!"

"My, aren't those your most precious possessions, young mistress? Is it all right for you to give them away?"

"Yes, it's f-fine... I'm all... all right..."

No, it's not fine, and I'm not all right!

Inwardly crying, I wrapped the box tightly and headed to the couch to accept the tea and snacks Violet had prepared. I squeezed my eyes shut and held out the box.

"Happy belated birthday, Rion. Please take care of my babies for me."

"Thank you! I shall work hard with this gift you have given!"

Wait, what? You're actually going to use them? The barrel is made of wood! If they get stained with ink... you won't be able to remove it...!

No... these pens are out of my hands now. I gave them to Rion, so I shouldn't interfere with how he wants to use them. It's not my place anymore... but...

...Sob!

"Glen! Take a break with me!"

I called for Glen to assuage my aching heart a little bit quicker. *If I have Glen by my side and squeeze and smoosh him for a bit, I'll soon forget letting my babies go.*

With that thought in mind, I called out for Glen, expecting him to join me from the side room, but there was no response... He didn't even answer.

"Glen! My darling fiancé! Let's have some tea before we continue working!"

Weird... Why isn't he answering?

"Glen...?"

"Leave him be," Rion said. "Lord Glen must be busy."

"It's strange that he won't even respond, though."

Is he sick?

Worried, I stood up. Rion clung to my arm, saying that Glen probably didn't hear me because he was so busy. *But if he's that busy, that's an issue in itself. I'll take some of his workload since I've got more time on my hands.*

Lightly shaking Rion off as he dangled from my arm, I went to Glen to suggest we fill our bellies with Violet's treats before continuing to work.

He was spinning his pen with the glummest face in the world, but thankfully, he didn't appear to have as much work as I had feared.

"You seem fine. Let's have some snacks first."

"..."

"Oh, would you like me to help you up? Hold my hand."

"No, thank you."

Oh my.

Are his matters so pressing that he can't accept my helping hand?

I glanced at his papers, wanting to help him if something had to be done immediately, but nothing seemed urgent.

Uhm... what was the matter, then?

"Your precious Rion is waiting for you. Please go back to your office."

"How could we enjoy those tasty snacks without you?"

"You normally pay no mind to me, so why are you acting this way? If I recall, you would not even let me touch those pens you gave him. You said they might get dirty."

"..."

Ah, he's sulking.

Yeah, now that I think about it, that did happen.

I came home excited that I had succeeded in buying the limited-edition set. Glen had asked me what it was and if he could take a look, but I didn't let him near them because the pens were too precious. I carefully displayed the set inside the cabinet instead.

I get why he's upset. Yeah, this was my mistake.

"I'm sorry. But what was I supposed to do? Rion wanted them so badly."

"Of course. You would get married to him if he threw a big enough tantrum, Lady Rosalite."

"Why would I marry him? He's my brother."

Did something just thump against the wall? Is it my imagination?

It wasn't—because Glen heard it too. He glanced at the wall and smirked.

Why does he seem to feel better now...?

"I see. Yes, he is your brother, so he will never get to marry you, even if it kills him."

"Of course. Who would marry their own brother? Never in a million years. And you know that you're the only one I've chosen as my husband, so why would you say that?"

"Is that so...?"

"Obviously. I'm almost finished with the wedding preparations, so don't you dare think about backing out. Our contract is stored in a safe, too. Death won't be the only punishment if you run away."

I'll chase you to the ends of the earth, clasp a collar on you, and drag you back home to bury you in work.

I looked Glen straight in the eyes, and a few more *thumps* sounded from the wall. I wanted to go and check what the sounds were, but Glen held out his hand.

"I suppose it can't be helped if you put it that way. I shall take a break."

"It's so hard to please you, my groom-to-be."

"We do not have to get married if you do not like that."

"No, of course I do. You're the best. My fiancé is the best!" I gave him three exaggerated hurrahs and held his hand to help him stand.

When I led him out into my office, I saw a fork and knife had been stuck into the wall.

"Lily, did you do this?"

Lily is super strong, and she's made holes in the wall before while trying to catch a bug, so she could probably do something like this.

When I asked her if the thumping noises were from her trying to catch a bug, Lily glanced at Rion and then back at me before nodding vigorously.

So, it was Lily, then.

"You should have called for me to catch it. You'll make holes in the wall again."

"Mnnggh... My apologies, young mistress."

Is she frustrated that she couldn't catch the bug? Why is she looking at Rion while on the verge of tears? What does Rion have to do with the bug in the first place?

"I have poured you a cup of tea," Rion said. "It should be the perfect temperature to drink right now."

"Thank you."

Hehe. What a thoughtful little brother he is.

I sat on the couch and patted the seat next to me so Glen could sit down. Rion was a good boy, and he had poured Glen a cup as well, so I didn't need to worry about anything else. I took a sip of black tea.

Mmm, this really is the perfect temperature. Now, let's see what kind of snacks we have today—

"Violet. Please empty my cup and pour me a fresh one," Glen said, without laying a finger on his teacup.

I bit into a warm scone. I guess I wasn't the only one confused as to why he was making Violet work twice, because Rion calmly voiced his thoughts as he sat across from us.

SEVENTY-SEVEN

"Why are you discarding a perfectly fine cup of tea? What if rumors spread that you are too harsh on the servants, Lord Glen?"

"It was too cold for my taste. Violet will understand, considering how much my stomach hurt the last time I visited the annex."

"It should not have been that cold," Rion protested. "I told you it was the perfect temperature."

"Well, what can I say? It was too cold for me."

"My sister is drinking it just fine. I am quite concerned with how much trouble she will go through in the future, since the person she is to marry is so finicky."

What the hell is going on...?

Glen and Rion were speaking as gently as a spring wind, smiling at each other, but I felt so uncomfortable.

I don't know why, but it's so awkward. I want to leave right now. I slumped my shoulders at the puzzling feeling and watched them carefully for a moment before stepping into the conversation.

"Lord Glen, the tea is really not that cold..."

"You stay out of this, Lady Rosalite."

Yeah, okay, sorry. Don't glare at me. That's scary.

I decided not to say anything else due to the undercurrent of pressure he sent my way. I sipped on some tea and munched on the scones.

As I sat there, quietly stuffing a whole scone into my mouth, Rion took my side, apparently finding me pitiable.

"You are quite peculiar, Lord Glen. Why are you venting your anger on my poor sister?"

"You are the peculiar one here, Lord Rion. This is not venting anger. I am protecting Lady Rosalite from any unnecessary unpleasantness."

"Whoa, what kind of imaginary enemy are you fighting, Lord Glen?"

"Haha. You know that better than I do, Lord Rion."

...I think I'm going to be sick.

I just wanted the three of us to chitchat with snacks. Should I run away? I didn't get to see the sun the past two days. I'll just say I'm going for a walk and leave.

"Aster! Let's go for a walk!"

"Yes, little miss."

"Hurry, hurry, hurry!"

Urging Aster on so I could get out of my office faster, I jumped into her arms. We put Rion and Glen's shouts about where I was going behind us and headed toward a newly developed promenade trail.

I'll have to work with those two once the new office is finished… Was my decision too rash?

Instead of taking the path by the estate park, Aster carried me in her arms to the promenade trail next to the Brown residence and the rabbit hutch. The duke had created the new trail purely to watch the rabbit, and sure enough, he was walking ahead of us with a pig leg in his hand.

I clambered down from Aster's arms. "It is good to see you look as healthy as ever, Your Respected Twinkling Star Grace."

The duke was alone, without Sir William, and he turned his head slowly to accept my greeting. "You're earlier than usual."

"I ran away."

"I figured."

Fascinating. How does he know everything?

I added that I had escaped from Asterion and Lord Glen, just in case the duke's guess was wrong, and he nodded as he said that he knew.

Seriously, that's amazing. How does he know?

"I heard that you're planning to have three desks in the new office, correct?"

"Yes, Your Grace."

"Place partitions between the desks, and make sure those two don't run into each other."

Why do you seem so familiar with this sort of situation?

I was about to ask him how he knew so much, quite amazed, but the duke quickened his pace with an unusually delighted look on his face, so I couldn't bring myself to interrupt.

The duke arrived at the rabbit hutch, which had been completed before the new office or the printing room. He pressed a little switch on the fence, announced his presence with the bell and called out brightly.

"Peter!"

Not long after, the huge rabbit hopped out of his hutch and rushed to the fence.

"Peter has scheduled meals," I said. "He'll get fat if you make a habit of feeding him in between."

"Who cares? It's just a tiny pig's leg."

"How is that pig leg tiny? You're the reason Jack worries that Peter isn't eating his actual meals."

"You're turning into William."

How could you say something so awful?

I was about to complain, but I stayed silent when I saw how happy he was. *He looks so cold, but he loves children and animals, strangely enough.*

He can tell the difference between identical twins, make children open up to him, and invite animals to approach him first...

*What is he? A D*sney princess? Is my duke a D*sney princess?*

"Rosalite! Dearest Rosalite! My daughterrr!"

Oh, damn.

I had wanted to chat with the duke as we watched Peter crunch on the pig leg, but the person who shouldn't have been there the most came closer.

Sir Sage dashed toward me, apparently not even noticing the duke was there until he came within a foot of us. Finally seeing the duke standing next to me, Sir Sage scowled.

The duke was scowling as well. "Why are you calling 'my' daughter 'your' daughter?"

The two men exchanged huffs and scoffs before each took a step back. I stood in the middle.

"Are you even aware she is your daughter?" Sir Sage replied.

"Answer my question first."

"Hmph. Rosalite grew up reading my academic papers. She admires and respects me. You could say she looks up to me as her mentor. Everyone knows mentors are almost always better than fathers."

"You pay rent to live here. Mentor? How laughable."

"I pay rent to Rosalite, not you."

"This is my house."

"It'll be Rosalite's house the second you die. You have a lot to say for a waning authority."

"It appears you wish to be executed for conspiracy against the aristocracy."

"What conspiracy? According to Rosalite, I'm totally on the level to rub shoulders with you. Who am I related to again, Rosalite? Those Northerners."

"Sir Sage is the cousin of the great-grandfather of Duke Noithram."

"Yes, exactly!"

I feel like the duke is glaring daggers at me, but it's probably just... not just my imagination...

"Whose side are you on, Rosalite?"

"Don't be daft. She's obviously on my side, the mentor she truly respects. Has she ever told *you* she respects you?"

"..."

No, stop looking at me and think. You know, just slowly recall the past, and you'll recall an incident when I told you I respected you. Probably.

"Not only that, but Rosalite told me she has high regard for me beyond respect. Have you ever heard her call you 'papa'? She's never even called you 'dad' before, has she? Well, that's what she calls me! You always torment her and shove piles of work at her. That's why she's never been able to call you her daddy!"

"…"

No, that isn't true either, dad! Think carefully. You've probably heard me call you dad here and there. I call you my duke dad pretty often when I talk to myself.

"That is not the case, Your Grace. You know how much I respect you, even if I do not tell you directly."

"Yet you still won't call me 'dad.'"

"And see this! Rosalite, dear, what did I discuss on page forty of *Lightning Magic Application: Volume II*?"

"Ah, you mean the part about nuclear fusion using quark-gluon plasma. It will become a source of energy once a possible safety device is invented, but that is unfeasible with the current technology and dangerous because someone might abuse it to blow up an entire town. Thus, I believe that every available copy of the book must be recovered and destroyed, my dear mentor."

"See! Look at that! She remembers every single thing I've ever written, down to the last letter!"

Shit! I answered reflexively because I spent half a century using that book as a reference for my dissertation!

I wanted to emphasize the part where I said every single book should be destroyed from this world, but it seemed the duke didn't have the headspace to catch that.

The duke thought long and hard, trying to think of something to beat Sir Sage with. I watched him for a moment, hoping he wouldn't have to suffer more heartbreak.

I shut my eyes tightly. "I apologize, Your Grace. The *Compendium of Laws* that you have revised is too thick, and the letters are too small."

The duke looked as if the world had crashed down upon him, and Sir Sage held his nose high in the air as though he had won.

But what could I do? The letters in that book are smaller than the Bible's, the pages are super thin, and I could probably break open someone's skull if I whacked them with it.

I had lived at the duke's estate for decades, but I could never dare to memorize the whole thing. All I could do was guess where a certain subject matter was written...

You're probably the only one in the entire country who's memorized that book.

"...This isn't over."

Wait, you got your ass handed to you by Sir Sage, so why are you mad at me, Your Grace?

The duke glared at me and turned around to leave. Sighing, I ruffled Peter's fur as he crunched away at the pig leg. *Just where the hell can I rest in peace on this enormous estate?*

"Why is that man picking a fight with his innocent child?"

"It's because of you, Sir Sage."

"What did I do?"

Never mind if you don't know. What will I get out of grumbling at you?

Anyway, if Sir Sage was pressed enough to run all the way here from the Magical Research Facility when he saw me, doesn't that mean he has something to say to me? When I asked him as much, Sir Sage gasped, suddenly remembering the business he had forgotten.

"I haven't given you your wedding present yet."

"Yes, you haven't."

"Remember the four-wheeled vehicle I was telling you about before? Well, I made another little toy while I was working on that."

Ooh, I'm interested. Nothing you call a toy ends up just being a simple toy.

I hastily dragged Sir Sage all the way to the new garage I had built for him. Copper wires and mana crystals littered the ground like trash, along with steel sheets, bolts, and nuts. In the corner of the garage where Sir Sage was pointing, I saw something familiar.

That's...!

"A S-Segw*y!"

"What in the world is a Segw*y? This is an 'automatic zoom-zoom.'"

What? That name sucks.

I couldn't hide my horror at Sir Sage's terrible naming abilities, but I quickly smoothed my expression over by hopping onto the Segw*y.

I could feel the mana crystal buzzing, urging me to let energy flow into it as soon as I grabbed the handles. As I transformed my mana into electricity, the wheels began to roll. Riding the Segw*y at a speed similar to a person running, I went around the outside of the garage and braked in front of my darling papa.

"Papa, you're the best!"

"I'm glad you like it, but you only call me 'papa' when there's something in it for you."

"That's not the case! I could never dare to call my highly respected Sir Sage 'papa' on an ordinary day!"

"Well, that can't be helped, then, can it? Call me 'papa' whenever you feel like it."

Yes, sir. Thank you, sir. You're the Alain Kingdom's brilliant genius!

Papa was elated even by my half-assed compliments and told me to run along and do my thing. Then he headed back to his research facility. *Aster isn't interested in the Segw*y, but Jack will probably be super jealous. I should only ride this to work when Aster's on the job.*

Later, I stopped by the dining hall for a coffee and drank it as I headed back to my office.

I hope Sir Sage never recovers his memories. If I keep him holed up here and use him for another fifty years, I'll probably catch up to twenty-first-century technology without a problem.

HIS ROYAL HIGHNESS WANTS TO BE ASKED OUT—THE CRAZY CHICKEN COUNTING FESTIVAL

I threw the Automated Return System-Enhanced Rosalite Roxburg Mach II out the window.

That ghastly thing keeps returning to me no matter how many times I throw it away. It's unspeakably irksome. What can I do to destroy it?

To be honest, destroying the actual Rosalite Roxburg is the more pressing matter, but I don't have the strength for that. Goddamn House of Roxburg.

That woman had been a thorn in my side since the very first time we met. When she followed her father to the palace to strike against the Crown Princess, she'd practically been a baby, and I had spoken to her for the first time after my installation ceremony as the Crown Prince. She had asked me a few questions and then returned home, after looking at me like I was the most pathetic thing in the world.

Not long after that, I received all sorts of medicinal herbs that were good for mental development. Inside the package was a letter that read, "For the Crown Prince of a nation to have an intellect so low it is impossible for him to perform everyday tasks is a matter of great concern, and you must at least now strengthen your brain."

The letter was written on recycled paper, as if to say I wasn't even worth the expense of proper stationery. I seriously considered leaving the palace at once to storm the duke's estate and strangle Rosalite Roxburg to death.

She didn't appear in front of me for a long time afterward, but then she started visiting the palace to hound me to get married. When I told her that she should take care of her own marriage issues before pestering me about mine, she actually brought her soon-to-be husband.

Is he completely insane? What was he thinking, getting engaged to that woman and choosing to marry her? Is he being blackmailed? Probably. He wouldn't think of marrying her if his life weren't on the line. That poor man.

"Damn it."

It's back so soon.

I watched the Rosalite Roxburg Mach II that I had flung outside struggle to clamber through the window. I lifted it nicely with both hands before catapulting it out the window again. Then I checked the list of luggage I was to take.

All this bothersome work is because of that woman, too. I had been forced to choose a random marriage prospect because she pushed for me to have an arranged meeting, and now, I was forced to go to an island. I marked the list the servants had brought me and turned to look at the bookshelf.

I should take the shelf as emotional support. Since that awful woman and her even more awful servants are coming along.

I removed a children's book from the collection. It was one that I had asked my nanny to read to me over and over again when I was a little boy, so the cover was very worn, but it was still precious to me. *I still remember the title embossed in gold.*

"The Blue-Ribboned Pirate"

It was an action tale about a noble girl from a ruined family who dressed like a boy to board a pirate ship and go on adventures in the ocean.

The image of the girl, gazing at the stars with a rum in her hand, a song on her lips, and a blue ribbon in her silver-haired ponytail, was still deeply etched into my heart. She was like my first love.

Ah, just hugging this book against my chest makes me feel better. I know it's only for a few days, but I'll have to see that terrible woman from morning until night. I'm so glad I have this book with me.

I added the storybook to the list of items I was to take and finished getting ready for bed.

As I placed a sleep shade over my eyes and tucked my sheep doll under my arm, I recalled the woman, who I hoped would never appear in my dreams, rubbing her lips over it.

Right, I sent her bread crusts in revenge, and she sent me that fucking automated return doll.

The Roxburg family forced me to become the Crown Prince, and I still hand-picked the ingredients to personally make and send her food. She should lay flat on the ground and thank me for it, not retaliate!

Seriously, nothing works out when I get tangled up with the Roxburgs. I wonder if an unnatural death awaits her tonight.

I wish she'd disappear. With all my heart, I really wish she would. I pray the entire House of Roxburg will be exterminated overnight so they have to live on the streets.

Of course, my hopes would never come to fruition, but I prayed with all my might anyway.

I didn't sleep well.

It was one hundred percent Rosalite Roxburg's fault.

Who would have thought I wouldn't be able to sleep because I was so pissed off thinking about her? She always made me sick with anger, so I often fell asleep with the help of alcohol. But I never expected to spend the entire night praying for her misfortune.

This is probably just proof that I'm worried about today's arranged meeting. Though I had chosen a marriage prospect who had nothing to do with the four duchies, I was still suspicious of her.

Her handwriting had changed in the middle of our correspondence, as though the writer had changed, and sometimes there were droplets of a strange liquid scattered across the letters.

I felt uneasy for several reasons, but it was still better than an arranged meeting with someone chosen by the four duchies. And it was a million times better than meeting a woman the Roxburgs pushed upon me.

I live my life with stress-induced ulcers because of that woman. My life will be over if I marry someone she has influence over. I'll die of some mental and emotional disorder brought on by repressed anger. Not only that, but she'll also have control over my kids, too.

Never. I'll die before that happens.

With only that determination keeping me afloat, I headed to the harbor. My mood soured like old milk when I saw Rosalite Roxburg flouncing around, all excited because she hadn't seen the sun in a few days. I had no choice but to greet her. I had to put a stop to her disgraceful behavior.

"My, if it isn't the lady of the Roxburg duchy? I thought you were just a little commoner girl in that garb."

"You're wearing a lot of clothing for this warm weather, Your Highness. Are you sure you're not sweating from every swaddled pore? Why don't you lift up your arms so I can check?"

"My sweat glands know how to read the room, unlike you, Lady Rosalite. They are not as unmanageable as you are. I'm sure your fiancé would say something if he saw you prancing around with so much skin showing just because you are warm."

"My fiancé is kind and sweet, unlike you, Your Highness. So, he only tells me nice things."

"Is he on such a tight leash already? That poor man."

"As will be your future if this meeting goes well, Your Highness."

"Hmph. There is no way I would let that happen."

I speak to her out of the goodness of my heart, and she's picking a fight again. Why can't I ever end a conversation on a good note with that woman?

I had been polite enough to the woman, so I whipped my head around and boarded the royal ship prepared by the Crown. Once onboard, I saw that a luxury sailboat with a House of Roxburg flag was taking in tourists. The sailboat was bigger than the royal ship and far grander. It seemed to be the latest model with an emergency power system.

Is she trying to brag that her family has more financial resources than the Crown? For what other reason is it docked right when my ship is about to leave?

The money for one of those sailboats could probably fund the second prince's shabby palace three times over and still have money left. Yet she fiercely opposed the reconstruction, saying there wasn't enough money to fix the palace. When I finally managed to reconstruct the place to make it livable for a human being, she dug up some secret corruption that happened during the construction process to toy with me.

"..."

Just don't think about her. My stomach hurts already.

It's all karma anyway, so who am I to blame? I used to live at the second prince's palace that my little brother was currently living in.

I was shunted aside by the Crown Princess and had to live like I was dead, barely receiving proper support. I was only able to leave the damn wreckage the day before I was made Crown Prince.

I used to wonder if I was going to live the rest of my life in those moldy, derelict ruins. Then one day, someone came to tell me that the Crown Princess was unfit to succeed the throne. They threw all the responsibilities onto my shoulders and transferred me to a new palace. A parade of tutors cycled in and out of my quarters regardless of the hour.

If I had asserted my authority during that time to fix the second prince's palace, my little brother wouldn't be stuck in there and suffering from asthma.

"..."

Wait. This is the Roxburg family's fault too, no matter how I think about it.

I'll get my revenge on you Roxburgs. You only see royalty as a cogwheel that turns this country. Throwing away a gear that didn't turn to their taste was easy, and replacing it was just as easy. If the gear didn't fit, all they had to do was pound it down and reshape. Telling me it was my responsibility, even pressuring me day after day to have children.

Just what am I to them? Do they even consider me an actual human being? Well, I know Rosalite Roxburg treats me like a breeding horse. She comes over whenever she pleases, just to tell me I don't have to get married as long as I go and make babies some other way.

You can't make babies on your own, you damn woman!

Whew... calm down. I'm here to meet Princess Irini today, so I need to reserve my energy.

I arrived at the island and watched Rosalite work excitedly with one of my servants before I went to prepare for my afternoon nap.

Unpacking my luggage only took a quarter of the time it took to pack back at the palace. That woman is so crazy about efficiency that it makes me sick. Ugh, the way she scratched her head as she checked the people entering the island and the luggage being unloaded... so undignified. And who was that man next to her wearing that strange mask? I swear, there isn't a single decent human being around her.

When I woke up from my scheduled nap, I learned that Princess Irini and her people had arrived.

I was about to step out to meet her when I was told that the first Imperial Prince of the Largole Empire was also here. *Rosalite Roxburg is so fussy about everything, but what the hell is she doing? Is she even dealing with it?*

My stomach ached. Why do I have to meet the man first in line for the imperial throne face-to-face during my arranged meeting with a marriage prospect? He said he was here lightheartedly, so I should treat him the same, but how am I supposed to just accept what he says?

Above all else, Rosalite will probably laugh at me if I relax because of what he said. She might tell me she's worried about my intellect and bring in an esteemed doctor this time.

I tried to hold myself together, but Princess Irini suddenly dropped to her knees at my feet and burst into tears.

Then she looked at my face and ran to the bathroom to vomit.

I was terrified.

Rosalite Roxburg was the only person I could depend on.

When I came to my senses, I found myself lying on the bed in my room with my arms wrapped around my storybook.

I don't know how the day went. I remember clutching at that woman and begging her to do something, and then... I think I went for a walk in the garden with the princess...

"..."

It's no use. I can't remember what happened afterward.

I opened my emotional support book and gazed at the pictures inside. The blue-ribboned pirate was as awesome and beautiful as always.

"Your Highness, someone from the House of Roxburg wishes an audience."

"Who is it?"

"It is Lady Rosalite's guard."

So, it's either the one in white or black. Happy that she gave me an excuse to rail at her for sending someone so late at night, I allowed the guard to enter.

The guard in black bowed in greeting and went straight to the point. "We found a corpse. I want to organize groups to patrol the area, so can I do as I please?"

"Does the guard of Lady Roxburg have no inkling of etiquette? And why is your speech so unrefined?"

"If you've got a problem, talk to the little miss. I'm a free man with the right to free expression."

That woman has no manners, which is probably why her aides are all rude and uncouth as well.

I told him to do whatever he wanted with the corpse or whatever and ordered him to kindly get lost.

The man, however, didn't leave the room for some reason and simply stared at me.

"What? I thought you were busy."

"Apologies. I saw something familiar."

Something familiar? I followed his downward stare. *Is he talking about the book I'm holding?*

"Do you mean 'The Blue-Ribboned Pirate?'"

"Is it really that book? Wow, talk about memories. I used to like that book when I was a kid."

You know this book when only three hundred copies have ever been printed? I've never met anyone else who's read it before.

"Ahem. I suppose you aren't that unsophisticated."

"It had lots of pictures. The main male lead's real pretty, too."

"It's a girl. A girl dressed as a boy."

"Is that right...?"

"It's about the only daughter of the ruined House of Pildin. She's ten years old in the beginning, twelve in the middle, and sixteen at the end. She has long, silver hair, and her favorite shoes are waterproof boots that come up to her knees. Are you sure you read this book?"

"You remember it to a creepy extent."

"Well, obviously. I still read it occasionally."

Disrespectfully enough, the man regarded me with pity before asking to be excused. *I want to keep him here and punish him, but I guess I'll have to let him go since he's got more important things to do to keep me safe.*

"…"

Hang on. A corpse… Does that mean someone died here?

As I expected, someone had died, and I spent night struggling to sleep.

All I had to do was focus on Princess Irini since dealing with dead people and finding the culprit was Rosalite Roxburg's job, but I wasn't happy about having grown men and women sleep in the same room.

I was in shock when I discovered that Rosalite Roxburg, that impudent, arrogant woman who encompassed everything bad in this world, did not see me as a man. Not even a little.

What did she mean when she said it wasn't right to view the relationship between a ruler and a subject as one between a man and a woman? I'm clearly a full-grown man. I swear, those Roxburgs are skilled at offending people.

Disgruntled, I spent more time than usual washing up and then decided to eat something since I was going to be at the dining hall anyway. That woman had thrown a fit about needing everyone to gather there in the morning. When I arrived, I saw something appalling.

Rosalite Roxburg had her hair tied up in a ponytail with a blue ribbon, and she wore a shirt and pants. To top it all off, she even had on shiny, knee-high boots.

"...What is with your getup?"

"We are in the midst of an emergency. I hope you will graciously understand my wish to dress comfortably in these circumstances, Your Royal Highness."

"Did your guard with the strange mask tell you?"

The woman didn't respond, but I knew what was going on. Her guard must have told her after he visited my room.

He probably told her to dress like that because I like "The Blue-Ribboned Pirate."

"..."

Wait, why is this woman going out of her way to dress in a manner that I like? Why? Don't tell me...

"...!"

It suddenly came to me. If it were true, I could understand every confusing thing that had happened before. Each piece of the puzzle was falling into place.

Rosalite Roxburg... is in love with me!

It was true. She grumbled about my intellect, but she sent me medicinal herbs for my health. The only excuse she had to come talk to me at the royal palace was to talk about marriage. Even though she pretended she made that doll to torment me... why would she spend so much money and effort on a doll if she weren't interested? Not to mention, that doll looked freakishly like Rosalite Roxburg. It had clearly been made by a master craftsman. Just making the doll would have cost a fortune.

That woman wasn't someone who would use money for no reason. I knew that best because I'd watched her all this time.

But harassing someone she likes... she's not a goddamn ten-year-old.

...Now that I think about it, she's quite a bit younger than I am. I had forgotten because I normally didn't have the opportunity to consider that.

Ah, I get it.

This woman must have had feelings for me all this time. Since when, though? Was it from the beginning? Did she fall for me the first time she met me? Well, I was handsome enough when I was young for a lot of girls to fall in love with me at first sight. Was she just one of the poor girls who fell for my good looks?

I couldn't tell if my food was going down my mouth or my nose because of this sudden realization, but Rosalite, the one who was in love with me, was nonchalantly eating smoked ham like all was fine.

I didn't know what she was thinking as she picked fights and insulted me as usual, all the while praising the first Imperial Prince, and that put me in a bad temper.

I decided to stop eating and just leave.

"Where do you think you are going without finishing your breakfast?!"

"How am I supposed to force food down my throat in this situation? I do not have nerves of steel like the lady of the Roxburg duchy!"

"You won't get smarter if you skip breakfast!"

That damn intelligence quip again! Is that woman unable to have a conversation with me without belittling my intellect?!

She should find ways to be loved by the person she likes instead of acting so coarsely. That's probably why she can't find anyone to marry her unless she threatens them.

When I left the dining hall, muttering to myself, Princess Irini dashed after me and asked me to please rescind my anger.

I spoke with her for a moment, drank some tea, and then found myself tied to my bed.

I was deeply surprised by the fact that the princess was straddling me, fully ready to rip off my clothes and take me for all I was worth, but when she told me about her true identity, I accepted it meekly.

Honestly, I had a feeling this was the case.

The splatters on the letters were blood no matter how I looked at them, and what was surely Princess Irini's handwriting up until a point had suddenly turned into awful-looking scribbles in the later letters.

The self-proclaimed dark mage blathered on about how she had sneaked into the imperial palace when she heard the news that Princess Irini was coming to see me for an arranged meeting. She killed the real princess, took her face skin, tricked those around her with mental manipulation magic, and succeeded in coming this far.

She went on and on about how she had no choice but to kill Princess Irini's direct maidservants yesterday and this morning because she was worried that she might get caught. But I was neither shocked nor impressed.

This wasn't the first time I'd met someone like this. It had been even worse before I became Crown Prince. There was no one to protect me back then, and I lived in a ramshackle joke of a palace with no security.

I always had to fight through every single tribulation alone. But this time around, I wouldn't have to do everything by myself. Even if I didn't call for her, Rosalite Roxburg would notice that something was off and come find me to ensure my safety. She'd do anything to keep me safe. Even if I were to discreetly meet with an imperial princess behind locked doors, she'd ignore everything and barge in.

See? That woman would bust through the entire place, regardless of the maids out front, just to protect me.

The impudent and arrogant woman with a horrible personality, who only knew how to insult and nag me, dealt with everything as promptly as I had expected. She freed me from my bonds and placed the Rosalite Roxburg Mach II in my arms as she explained that it had followed me to the island. Then she went to make preparations to return to the mainland.

Creepy little doll. You even crossed the ocean to follow me?

Now that I knew she loved me, gazing at her spitting image made me feel rather fond of the doll. I supposed this thing and that woman were kind of cute when they kept their mouths shut and stayed still.

I rubbed the doll's head as I thought about ways to make Rosalite Roxburg stop loving me. Her feelings for me were commendable, but I had zero intentions of getting married to a pestering woman who would keep me under her thumb.

"…"

But…

"..."

...why is she getting married to another man if she loves me?

PART VIII:
LIFE #22 (ROSALITE, TWENTY-ONE YEARS OLD, PART I)

I struck a combative pose as I faced Luke.

We were just about to dance the traditional tango of the imperial family of the Largole Empire. I couldn't help but be determined because of my past resentment at not being able to do this dance, and because both of us could get seriously hurt if we didn't dance in harmony.

Hmph. I can't believe he kept these exciting moves to himself! Foul little boy. What would I have done if I hadn't learned the dance from the first Imperial Prince?

"Must you do this dance, Lady Rosalite? It is not too late to call it quits."

"Quiet. Why do you think I've been summoning you to practice with me for the past month?"

"To torture me and make me walk home drenched in rain, since you call me over only when the weather is terrible. And all that because you have a grudge against me for not teaching you this dance before."

"Yes, that's true, too."

Wow, quick catch.

I was upset he hadn't taught me the imperial tango and hoped he'd have a hard time returning home, which was why I'd only been scheduling my meetings with Luke on days when thick, black clouds covered the sky.

And that's why the sky outside now is writhing as though it might pour torrents of rain at any moment. The orchestra exclusive to the House of Roxburg had a hard time preparing as well due to the humidity. String and woodwind instruments weren't in the best condition on humid days like this.

But that hardly matters to me because I'm practically tone-deaf!

I would never notice if the notes were half a key sharp or flat, but the concertmaster always strove for perfection and spent his time dehumidifying the dance hall as much as he could before using it.

That's why there were bowls filled with salt all over the floor, as well as countless candles all around. Honestly, it was kind of stuffy.

"Are you ready, Luke?"

"Are you? Please do not hurt yourself and cry about it later."

"If I get hurt, it's your fault."

"This is precisely why I didn't want to come!"

Hahaha! And what are you going to do about it? You need to get your ass here when the young mistress of the duchy calls.

"Why are you dawdling, concertmaster?! Drop the beat, I say!"

I ordered the concertmaster to begin and clapped my hands to set a rhythm. Luke stomped over to me and pulled me so roughly toward himself that I couldn't help the gasp that escaped my lips.

"Don't let your ulterior motives seep into the dance."

"My apologies, Lady Rosalite. I am deathly resentful at the moment."

"You shouldn't have burst into the spa and shoved your business card in my face if you were going to be resentful about something as trivial as this."

"That was one of the best things I have done in my life."

Then don't be resentful.

I grabbed Luke's shoulder and twirled round and round, even adding an aerial kick in my excitement, and followed his lead.

Luke held my back as he helped me cartwheel backward, and I timed my landing before quickly approaching him again.

I hadn't been able to pull this move off with Lukius, but I finally succeeded in doing the backward cartwheel. And it felt like my years' worth of frustration had washed away.

"By the way, Luke..."

"Yes?"

We moved enthusiastically, and I let out a grunt as I grabbed Luke's waist to help him jump. *Honestly, this really doesn't seem like a lady's dance move.*

"I didn't notice when I was dancing with Prince Lukius, but why do I have to use my strength so much when I dance with you?"

"That is because I have only done this dance with men."

You've only done this sexy dance with men? Don't suddenly burst out of the closet like that. It's too shocking.

Well, it's easy for me to accept him for who he is because I already know his type.

"I see... Yeah, that makes sense!"

"I have always thought so, but the way you respect others' preferences is remarkable."

Who cares as long as you do your job well? I mean, Rion plays with dolls at his age. Being close with men isn't even an issue.

Hmm, now that I think about it, Rion is already twenty. This time of year always scares me. He dies like a fly whenever he hits twenty, you know? I haven't even figured out what his wish is yet.

"By the way, Lady Rosalite. Isn't it your wedding soon?"

"It is. I'll send you an official invitation once our rings are ready. You're coming, aren't you?"

"Of course. Who would help pay for your wedding if I do not attend?"

That means you'll be coughing up some congratulatory dough in addition to the gift you sent before, right?

Greatly pleased by Luke's words, I twirled in place and grasped his lower back. I had him lean back as if to lay him down and then used my other hand to grab his wrist and hold him up. Luke wrapped an arm around my shoulder and grunted as he struggled to stay in position, using all the strength he had in his legs and back as he protested.

"This position is too difficult for me."

"As it is for me."

"May we stop now?"

"Yes, let's do that."

I drew in a sharp breath as I pulled his waist upright, and Luke barely managed to regain his balance. Once he straightened up, he fell back into rhythm and continued to dance.

"I wonder how our dear Luke has such a strong lower back, hmm?"

"That is sexual harassment."

"I don't know who'll take you, but your partner is a lucky guy."

"That is sexual harassment!"

Duh, I know that!

Why do kids these days yell so much? I can hear everything just fine without the hollering. It's not like I'm going deaf or anything.

"Speak softly. I can hear you just fine."

"You failed to listen to me when I spoke calmly, so I figured you must have a problem with your ears."

"You always have to get the last word in, don't you, you plucky child."

"How would I ever dare to own a business in the Duchy of Roxburg without that kind of nerve?"

That's true.

Luke's words were valid, and I wasn't at all upset by the way he talked back. *Why would I be upset? He's endearing. Young people should have ambition. Being a tad impolite because of that is just charming.*

"Concertmaster! Vivace!"

"Are vivace and forte the only two terms that the Roxburgs know?!"

Why is he all crumpled?

The concertmaster, who was the greatest violinist in the entire Roxburg estate, suddenly bellowed at me when I requested a quicker tempo. *Seeing how he's been so grumpy since a while ago; I'm guessing he'd been called by the duke before he was summoned by me.*

"Why are you grouching at me when the duke's the one who wore you out?!"

"Because you are easier to deal with, Lady Rosalite!"

This is why I don't like artists. Always imposing their pride, even if it kills them.

Well... not that I can kick him out because he's the only one who leads the orchestra to my and the duke's liking.

He's probably acting like that because he knows that. What, is playing the violin so well such a big deal?

Yeah, I guess it is, but still...

"All right, fine! Vivace! Vivace! Concertmaster!"

The concertmaster fumed, but repositioned himself all the same and moved his bow.

Ahhh, yes! That's what I'm talking about! I grabbed Luke's hands and repeatedly danced back and forth as the tempo increased, totally elated.

After a wild bout of dancing, Luke was gasping for air and completely drained, and the concertmaster herded the orchestra out for a drink, saying that they were going to take a break.

I wiped the sweat from my face with the cool towel Violet had brought over, letting out a satisfied moan.

Ughhh, this feels nice. My muscles are finally relaxing. I hadn't been able to move around much lately, and my body had been creaking like an old door.

"Do you want to wash up before you go? I'll have someone ready a bath."

"*Huff*...No...thank you...*Huff*...I have...*Huff*...work to do."

Oh right, you're super busy, too.

He always comes to the estate to hang out with me when I ask, even if he's busy, and he'll probably gift me a whole lot of cash for my wedding. Perhaps I should give him a present on his way home.

Let's see... Should I let slip the details of the streetcar that I'm planning to build? Or should I tell him about the redevelopment of the slum area near the Edanelli border—

Boom.

Just as I was debating which information he might like best, Luke suddenly flinched and shuddered.

His wide eyes stared once at the scenery outside of the window, and contrary to his initial surprise, he calmly collected himself and deftly whipped out the tablecloth from a nearby table.

Once he elegantly removed the white tablecloth without disturbing the flower vase or any other ceramics resting on top, he squirmed as he covered himself with it and quietly crouched onto the floor.

"What are you doing?"

"Please wait a moment, Lady Rosalite. I shall leave once I have calmed myself."

"Right... Do as you will."

I waited patiently, thinking that he would come out from under the tablecloth at any moment, but Luke seemed to have no desire to reveal himself no matter how long I waited.

I don't know what he's doing that for, but it's awkward for me to just wait out here. I think I'll squeeze in there with him.

"Scooch over a little."

I whipped right under the tablecloth and settled down next to him. Luke was scrunched up with his face buried in his knees and his hands over his ears, quite unbefitting for a man his height.

"Do you feel ill? I can call for a physician if you don't feel well."

"No, I'm all right. I shall be fine if I stay like this."

Hmm... While I knew about his past due to the novel, I couldn't rashly ask him about it.

Luke's life wasn't your usual hot mess. The suffering he had undergone from the time he lived alone with his mother to the time he was taken in by the House of Shatel couldn't be summarized in a few pages of a book.

I'm pretty sure there are parts that have been omitted, and he's probably been through terrifying incidents that I don't know about.

"Hold my hand."

"I'm sorry...?"

"It's less scary when someone's beside you."

This method was quite effective when Jack was freaking out about ghosts, too. I don't know what he's so frightened of, but holding someone's hand makes it far less scary. Above all else, Luke would be able to rely on me because I'm not at all afraid of what frightens him.

"Will you just listen to me?"

I snatched Luke's hand into both of mine when he hesitated. His hand was as cold as a block of ice, apparently having been terrified. *He was so sweaty from dancing a moment ago, and now his hands are freezing. Tsk.*

"I don't know what scared you so much, but it's going to be all right because I'm here. And let me know if anyone bothers you."

"You are the one who bothers me the most, Lady Rosalite."

"Are you saying you were scared because of me?"

Luke burst out laughing at my exaggerated tone. His hand also began to warm up little by little, as if he were calming down.

"I am reminded of incidents that happened in the past whenever the weather is foul, which is why I end up like this. Thank you for your consideration."

"I see. It must be quite troublesome when you're alone."

"Are you not going to ask what happened?"

"Who cares about what happened to you?"

"That is true. It is none of Lady Rosalite's concern what kind of dung pit a lowlife like I have rolled around in."

"Tsk, tsk. You're being sarcastic again."

Manners, manners!

Still, his snark was proof that his fears had subsided considerably, so I stayed under the tablecloth with him for a little while longer. Once I confirmed that the rumble of thunder had died down, I carefully crawled out from beneath it.

He had crawled underneath the cloth when the thunder boomed loudly, so that sound was probably the cause.

"It appears there will be heavy rainfall for a while, so stay here until it stops raining. I'm sure you'll be bored while you wait, so help me out with my work."

"You certainly know how to exploit me in all sorts of ways."

"Uh-uh. I'm making you work for your own good."

About ninety percent of the documents I had to stamp today were useless bits of work that I had to do, but there were a few important ones in between. Like papers on the streetcar plans or documents that could help one speculate about the reorganization of Roxburg distributions.

I was planning on telling him about those things as a gift anyway, so stamping some documents in my place would be a good thing for everyone all around.

I held Luke's hand to help him up and hummed on my way to my office. As we left the dance hall and climbed some stairs, Luke suddenly asked me a question, as though he realized something was strange.

"Your office is that way, is it not?"

"We moved the office."

I had all the desks and stuff transferred to the new office because the office was completed not too long ago.

Nowadays, Rion showed up more often to help with work because he had completed all of the basic schooling and training. All he had to do was do physical training with his tutor.

I honestly don't know what's so fun about work that makes him come in every day, though.

"Hehehe. Don't die of shock when you see the office."

The architect that you introduced to me renovated the office splendidly and made it so efficient and futuristic!

Personally, my heart nearly stopped because I thought I was back at my old company from my old world when I first walked in through the doors, but it was still amazing, nonetheless. *How does that architect do it? It's a mystery to me, but society would call someone like him a genius.*

"Da-da-da-la-da."

Obviously, no one would understand the meaning of the song, but all that mattered was that I was excited, so I hummed a part of the chorus of a song from a house renovation reality show.

The moment the doors opened, we saw a spacious area and my neatly organized desk. Next to the desk was a garbage can with a built-in automatic paper shredder, which I had made with the money I ripped off from the king a while back.

And the CEO chair right before us is fitted with wheels! Made of polyurethane! I know, surprise! Polyurethane! That architect dude invented polyurethane on his own and was using it for his work! Isn't that insane?!

CHAPTER
SEVENTY-EIGHT

From what I heard; the architect was a fire mage. He was able to smell different materials and said inventing new alloys was easy for him, but I had no idea where he got his materials from.

Of course, this wasn't at all surprising because most fire mages were in this line of work. After all, most fire mages discovered their abilities because they came from a smithing household or worked at a blast furnace, and one day they developed both fire tolerance and attributes.

Though uncommon, some chefs developed fire attributes as well. *And that uncommon man is the head chef at the royal palace of Alain.* Our kingdom was famous for seafood dishes, mostly because of him. *The way he uses his magic to cook dried seafood, making it so juicy and flavorful, is truly astonishing.*

"..."

Oh no. I'm starving. I'm already low on energy because of excessive exercise.

I turned left, knocked on the door to the maid's lounge, and asked for some snacks.

My newly renovated office no longer had a side room that the maids used. Now, Violet and Lily had their own lounge room.

The lounge was three times the size of the tiny side room in my old office and had a separate nap room as well. It was also supplied with simple cooking utensils, equipment, a couch, a table, and piles and piles of snacks and treats that we could eat whenever we wanted.

Even now, I didn't have to go all the way to the dining hall if I simply wanted to stave off my hunger for a moment. I could just make myself some toast.

No matter how many cookies and snacks I stocked in the lounge, they all disappeared on the days Aster came into work, but that was my cross to bear. *I mean, it can't be helped if it's Aster. I can't tell her to starve. All I can do is restock.*

With my mind full of the thought of filling my hungry belly, I held Luke's hand and led him to the guest couch. Rion and Glen, who hadn't even acknowledged me when I had returned, suddenly jumped to their feet at the sight.

How are they so synchronized when they can't even see each other because of the partitions?

"Lady Rosalite."

"Hm?"

Not only that, but they were both staring at Luke as though they were fascinated by him, and that seemed to make Luke uncomfortable.

He spoke to me and surreptitiously pulled the hand I was holding back toward himself.

"I think it will be better if you let go of my hand."

"Why?"

The moment the word came out of my lips, Rion stabbed a fountain pen into his desk.

If Rion had been the only one to react, I would have thought that perhaps Asterion was indeed solidifying his weird personality as he aged, but what surprised me was that Lord Glen pulled a sword out of his cane and stabbed it into the floor as well.

Rion is far superior when it comes to strength and fighting techniques, but I'm more scared of Glen. Why is that savage child hiding a damn sword in his cane?

"Because I do not wish to die young."

"I respect your wishes."

Yeah, I don't know what's going on, but I think shutting up and lying low is the best thing to do right now.

I hastily let go of Luke's hand, brought the documents that needed stamping to the guest tea table, and called for Jack Brown.

Jack, who probably would have been enthusiastically playing with his toys in the guard lounge, immediately popped out of his room and asked me what my business was with his usual swagger.

"Come here and hold Luke's hand for me."

"Why?"

"He's a bit anxious because of the bad weather."

Right as I finished speaking, thunder boomed outside, and lightning cracked, flashing brightly to light up the office. Jack quickly understood and switched places with me.

Holding tightly onto Jack's hand instead of mine, Luke stamped the documents in their respective places, then spoke to the man sitting next to him.

"Do all the people who grow up at the duke's estate turn out like this?"

"Like what?"

"Uh... you know... odd."

"Oh, that. Basically, yeah. Everyone needs to coordinate with the duke's common sense to make a living."

"Is the duke really that bizarre?"

"Generations of real bosses. According to my old man, the ancestors were even worse. The Roxburgs now at least communicate well and have much nicer personalities."

"Much... nicer?"

Maybe it's because they're little kids but making them hold hands helped them hit it off well.

I watched Jack flip the pages and Luke stamped down with a contented smile before I took my toast with chocolate jam back to my desk and sat down. My office design was so postmodern that it was kind of unnerving at times, but I liked the fact that I had a lot of storage space. The drawers were incredibly light, too. *How long has it been since I opened drawers with actual drawer runners?*

Anyway, I came here right after dancing with Luke. I hope I don't stink. I lifted my arm, took a whiff to make sure I didn't smell of sweat, and flapped my sleeve.

"..."

I'll just let that dry. Who cares if I smell? No one's going to sit close to me. I'll just tell the kids to plug their noses if they get too close.

As I took out a stack of papers I had been working on before going dancing from one of my drawers with a lock, I saw the almost full-grown Asterion approaching me.

The little kid that had grown strikingly compared to last year was now a head taller with even broader shoulders. He leaned in with his handsome visage, which still had a bit of his baby features left and spoke childishly to me.

"Sister, is it all right if I receive tomorrow's worth a day earlier?"

"Tomorrow's worth? Oh, are you talking about the warm hugs and whatnot?"

"Yes."

"I'm sorry, but I smell really bad right now."

"In my field of work, that is an additional award."

"..."

What the actual fuck?

"..."

N-no, no, no, no. I shouldn't think like that. Bad thoughts! Bad thoughts! Bad Rosalite for thinking bad thoughts!

I shook my head vigorously to get rid of the thought that had just crossed my mind and decided to coax Asterion instead. I had let him do as he pleased up until now because we were only in the presence of family, but requesting hugs while there were guests over was an issue.

I need to make him stop with the PDA now that he's older.

"Asterion."

"Why are you calling me that, sister? It is awkward."

"Can you... stop doing that?"

"Come again?"

Asterion looked genuinely surprised and then turned it on me by saying that we had a contract. He asked me how I could break the promise we had to hug for our entire lifetime.

Yeah, well, I mean, you're totally right, Asterion, but...

"You'll be twenty soon, and you're grown now. Uh, mentally and physically. We're both adults, so all the hugs and cuddles could be kind of... you know, for others to see."

"Why does that even matter? I am fine with it."

"You might be fine with it, but..."

The contract that I had signed was compensation for bringing in the child who was still studying to take my place, so continuing that contract with Asterion, who was now working in my office, was inappropriate.

I tried to lay out reason after reason, but he refused to accept any of them, so I had to make my decision.

I need to tell him the truth. Nothing but the truth will solve this problem.

All the hugs and cuddles were all right a long time ago, but now they were uncomfortable. Not only that, but he was huge now, and it felt like a boar ramming into me. His hugs made me gasp.

It was painful. Perhaps he thought he was still fun-sized because he always rammed into me with all his strength, so I was considering giving him a warning anyway.

I didn't tell him before because I didn't want to hurt his feelings, but I had a feeling I wouldn't get the chance to tell him if I didn't do it now.

"Asterion, listen to me."

"Yes, sister."

"Well…"

I took a deep breath and then stared right into his eyes. *I can say it. I can tell him the truth!*

"It's creepy."

There! I said it!

I closed my eyes in the end, but I still said it!

I was happy that I finally said what I had been wanting to say for the past few days, but Asterion's face twisted instantly.

I was about to suggest a different form of reward when I saw that his face blanched at the way I had said he was gross with my eyes squeezed shut, and even his lips trembled, but I couldn't say anything because of the screech that Jack let out.

He had been watching our conversation with bated breath, but now he was suddenly twitching with laughter as if he were having a seizure. The laughter continued as he banged the tea table with his fist and rolled around on the couch.

"Ahahaha! Ahaha! Eehehe! Heh! Hehe! Ahahack! She said… she said creepy! Haha! Bwahaha!"

Jack laughed and laughed like a mad man until he clutched at his chest and shoulders, saying he had cramps. And yet, he couldn't stop laughing, even though he was shedding tears of pain.

"Ahaha... Ow, my ribs! My ribs are about to break. Hah! Haha! Ehehehe! I'm gonna hurl! Blarghaha!"

Do I need to call a doctor?

As I watched Jack worriedly, Luke, who was still holding his hand, gently patted his back. *I suppose Luke wants to calm Jack down because he looks like he's in pain, despite being incredibly taken aback. What a kind child.*

"C-creepy...? Is that true, sister?"

"I'm sorry, but that's the truth."

"Ugh!"

I answered without pause because I had been holding it in for a while, and Rion made that noise he always makes and turned right around and left the office.

He left without finishing any of his work, but I decided to let him be since I could understand how shocked he was. Instead, I gathered the work Asterion had left behind and went up to Glen.

"Were you laughing, too?"

"I... uhm... apologize."

Watching him giggle as he covered his mouth with his hands to stifle his laughter was refreshing, but if the reason for his mirth was Asterion's unhappiness, then that wasn't something to praise him for.

I told him to maintain his dignity, scolded him that stabbing a sword into a floor wasn't a very nice thing to do, and then returned to my desk.

I'll have to go see Asterion when I'm done with work.

"Jack, walk Luke to the front gates when the weather clears."

Jack, still wheezing as if he had a hole in his lungs, nodded, while Luke grumbled about how I still didn't trust him even though so many years had passed.

Right, I don't trust you, but I'll also get in trouble if the duke finds out that I keep bringing you over.

After truthfully telling him so, I continued to finish up the work with Glen. It took quite a while without Rion's help. *I need to hurry up and coax him to come back.*

CHAPTER
SEVENTY-NINE

Once my work was done, I decided to go and find Asterion alone, but Jack threw a temper tantrum about wanting to come along with me. In the end, I headed to the annex with him in tow.

The front door of the annex where Asterion lived was smashed, and for some reason, there were holes in the brick walls, so I called some people over to repair the damage.

I could infer that Asterion slammed the doors on his way up, but is this annex so old that it would crumble just because a child slammed a few things?

Perhaps the duke and I had both been inattentive to Rion all this time. It had never crossed our minds to reconstruct the place he lived when it was as dilapidated as it was.

"I should scold the employees. Why wouldn't they report to me immediately if the building were this damaged?"

"Don't do that, little miss. You can't scold people for something so unexpected."

Unexpected, my ass! It's their fault for not taking care of the place.

Worried that Rion might be living in terrible conditions, I hurried upstairs.

When I knocked on his door and asked if Asterion was in, he replied that he was.

Thankfully, he wasn't upset enough to ignore me.

"Jack, I assume you have no wish to remain out here?"

"Ugh, and miss all the fun? No, ma'am."

"Then don't laugh like you did before."

"I'm so exhausted I can't laugh even if I want to."

Okay, good.

After giving Jack a firm warning, I opened the door and entered Rion's room. Rion was clearly still passionate about playing with dolls because dolls of varying sizes were displayed in a row. In one part of his display cabinet, there were perfumes with dates written under them.

...Hey, I think a few of those handkerchiefs over there are the ones I lost.

"You're not even trying to hide it anymore, are you? Gross. Just gross."

"Tsk! Jack, shut it."

Asterion is allowed to play with dolls. Why do you keep harping on about that?

I pinched and twisted Jack's lips and then approached the bed that Rion was slumped face-first in.

The bed looks tiny because he's grown so big over the past year. He should have asked me to get him a new bed if it doesn't fit anymore. He looks ridiculous with his feet hanging off the end.

"Asterion? Asterion, please sit up."

"Why do you keep calling me Asterion?"

"What should I call Asterion if not Asterion?"

"You used to call me Rion."

I'm sorry, but you're so enormous that I can't bring myself to call you that anymore. How should I, uh, say this... "Rion" gives me teeny-tiny cutesy vibes, you know?

"How could I speak to you like a child when you're an adult now, Asterion?"

"You just don't want to call me that anymore because it's creepy."

He's so quick-witted about things like this. I felt a prick of guilt but continued talking as if I weren't fazed.

"I fear I might have been too harsh with my words. What I meant by 'creepy' was... well..."

How do I gloss over this?

I thought hard about how to candy-coat the word "creepy" so it wouldn't hurt Asterion's feelings, but nothing popped into my head. Instead, I emphasized what I had said earlier.

"You're an adult now, aren't you? It doesn't look good for a grown man and woman to hug and cuddle whenever they feel like it."

"..."

"You know I'm about to get married. Even though we're close as siblings, those who do not understand our situation might spread rumors, and—"

"Does that mean..."

Jesus Christ, that scared me.

Asterion suddenly bolted upright from his facedown position and sat on his knees in front of me. *He's huge, even when he's on his knees. How did he grow so big? The mysteries of the human body, indeed. It's like he's grown half as much in both height and width compared to a year ago.*

"...you see me as a man?"

Huuuhhh?!

I think he missed the point... But I couldn't say no because Asterion was staring at me with sparkling eyes. Not to mention, he might sulk again and shove his face into his bed if I denied that.

"Uh... right? Mm-hmm. Yes. I see you as a man. Yup. That's it."

"Do you really?"

Okay, this is starting to get uncomfortable. Don't grab my hand and lean in so close.

But I can tell you anything you want to hear. Saying stuff doesn't cost anything.

"That's right. You're my dear brother but having a man who is a head taller than me come close makes me feel incredibly uncomfortable and shy."

"...You even feel shy?!"

"Yes, yes. It's awkward and embarrassing when a silver-haired, handsome man closes in for a hug."

"...Then does your heart pound as well?!"

"Uh-huh, my heart pounds as well."

It pounds in fear of unnatural death by falling on my back and cracking my head open when you ram me with your hugs. It pounds so hard that I feel like I might be paralyzed.

"Hehe, then that cannot be helped, can it? I shall be careful."

Clearly feeling much more cheerful, Asterion almost lunged at me for a hug but then jolted himself to a stop. He rubbed his cheek on my hand as an alternative. *Thank God he learns.*

We chatted for a while longer, and I told him I was going to send over new furniture and proceed with renovations before leaving.

I no longer had business at the annex because Asterion had assured me he was going to come back to work starting tomorrow. *I'll go up to my room, take a bath, and then take a nap.*

Before Jack and I parted ways outside of the annex, he asked me a strange question.

"Did you make a habit of digging your own grave?"

"Digging graves is your job, Jack."

"You don't understand metaphors, do you?"

What?! Of course, I do! I took intensive courses in Royal Alainian and years of literature classes!

At my indignant shout, Jack shrugged.

"You just keep living your life like that, then."

With those words, he left.

Hey! You need to at least explain what you're talking about before you leave. Jerk!

The wedding rings that I had been waiting for finally arrived the other day. I needed to flaunt my ring at the royal palace, but it had to be an appropriate size so it wouldn't be uncomfortable when I worked. That was why I had a two-carat teardrop diamond ring that wasn't too big or too small specially made.

I tried it on in secret without Glen, and the cut was absolutely stunning. It sparkled from every angle, and even those who didn't know its worth would at least understand that it was expensive. *No need to worry about rumors spreading about Glen being treated with contempt by the Roxburgs.*

Do you know how much money I used and how long I waited for a fully booked master craftsman to make this ring?

Highly satisfied with my purchase, which had been well worth the wait, I summoned Lem at once and made her print out the wedding invitations. She howled about how the duke had sucked her dry of mana when he called her in to make her send 2,401 chain letters to His Majesty the King, but that wasn't my problem. I decided to force her to continue her labor.

She should've just done her own work. Why did she get in between those two geezers? The duke probably messed with Lem and used her instead because he didn't want to waste actual ink on such stupid affairs. The fact that the duke spent some time with those ridiculous chain letters probably meant that he was quite invested in my wedding as well. He probably had to relieve stress by any means possible, and the poor king just became the prey caught in his trap.

Other people prepare months before their wedding, getting facials and going on trips, but what the hell am I doing?

"At least I get the day off tomorrow. Hehe."

I gulped down some coffee and scribbled away without rest. *I'll finish this all up and sleep all day tomorrow.* I've completed all preparations for the venue design, ushering guests, security, and the procession of events, so all I had to do was sleep tight and show up.

If I had known that the Roxburg-style wedding would be so complicated, I would have skipped the wedding ceremony and gotten a simple marriage registration instead.

What kind of wedding needs an orchestra, a dance hall, three dresses for the bride, a cook who can whip up a traditional Roxburg course meal, and a goddamn guest singer?

Not only that, but this wedding wasn't just for family and friends. Loads of people will attend, so every store in the duchy of Roxburg will celebrate our wedding with a special sale season.

It was extremely characteristic of the people of our lands to want to clear their inventory while clearing customers' moneybags when there were crowds of visitors at the duchy. However, this would most likely lead to a decrease in public safety and an increase in cretins, who would want to pilfer profits and taxes while they pocket supplies during the commotion. I'd have to go right back to work immediately after the wedding.

So unfair. In what world does a newlywed bride go to work in her wedding dress?

"Are you still here?"

I feel like I've heard that before.

As I sat there, pitying my miserable situation and staring out the dark window, Lord Glen Hoffen entered the office with a handful of files.

"Well, hello there, groom-to-be?"

"And hello there, bride-to-be."

"It doesn't sound right when we say it to each other. What is all that?"

Glen dropped the files onto his desk, avoiding my gaze and mumbling for a moment before explaining what he had brought in a small voice.

"I was thinking about perhaps... compiling statistics on the taxes paid to the duke's estate by the branch families..."

"You don't have to do that right now, do you? You just have to look over them before the end of the year."

"Yes, you are right, but..."

Glen mumbled hesitantly and eventually sat down at his desk and opened a file.

The way he was displaying his true value as the human Excel program was lovely, but it left me rather concerned. If he was making more work for himself today of all days, before our wedding...

"Marriage blues?"

"..."

"If you regret your decision to marry me, then—"

"That is not it."

Whew, what a relief. I was about to find your weakness and threaten you if you said you didn't want to get married. Controlling Glen is an easy task, and I have hostages I can use against him, so I wouldn't even break a sweat locking him up in our estate anyway, but I'm grateful he's entrapping himself with his own volition.

"It's just that I wonder if I am doing the right thing... I just have a lot on my mind."

"A lot on your mind?"

"We have never held hands in a romantic manner, nor have we ever been on a date, which begs the question about whether I am doing the right thing by getting married to a person when I do not even know if she is interested in me."

He must have had a lot on his chest, too.

Every single one of Glen's words pierced me like an arrow, and I couldn't do anything but clear my throat.

Pretending that the coffee I was drinking got caught in my airway, I coughed and thumped my chest a few times, wiped my mouth with a handkerchief, and then calmly spoke to him.

"Why are you thinking like that? Even if I do need a marriage partner, I'm not heartless enough to promise eternity with a man I don't even like."

"But it isn't an eternity. You know our contract renews every two years."

"Ahem! Cough! Hack! Ahem!"

He always has an answer to everything. Well, that is why I considered marrying him in the first place.

Glen's eyes were ice-cold regardless of how he was cornering me, so I had to say something. *Now is the time for my wit to shine!*

I set down my coffee mug and cleared my throat once more before speaking confidently. It was an answer that I had prepared ages ago in case he condemned me like this.

"How can you say we've never been on a date? We're always on a date in the office, aren't we?"

"..."

"..."

Why do you look even colder than before, Glen?

Glen wasn't looking at me like he was looking at another human being. He was staring at me like I was something less than an animal.

Flustered, I wondered what I had said wrong when he let out a deep sigh and opened another file, saying that he had to work.

"What would I expect from you, Lady Rosalite? Forget what I said."

He thinks I'm a total joke!

A little offended, I got up and headed toward Glen.

"..."

Yeah... I was about to head toward him.

But on the way there, I took a detour and stood next to the window, where I took several deep breaths. Then, I circled the middle of the office a few times before finally standing next to where he was sitting.

"Hey. Look here for a moment."

Ahem. If we can't go on a date right now, this is the only thing left to do.

CHAPTER EIGHTY

I grabbed Glen's face and leaned down as he gazed up at me without much thought. His eyes widened as my face drew closer, but he still didn't seem to understand what was happening.

No one was stopping us, and Glen wasn't resisting either, so our lips met easily. I didn't want to just end it with a smooch, so I nibbled on his lip and slowly pulled away. Glen's face was so red that it looked like it was about to explode.

"What do you think?! It's my first kiss!"

Embarrassed, I let out a boisterous laugh. *My face is burning. It's so hot here. Will my face be as red as his if I look into the mirror right now?*

Glen was silent, and standing next to him was awkward as hell, so I was about to head to the window to get some air when he reached out a hand to grab me.

He was even redder than before, and tears even sparkled in his eyes, but he gazed at me right in the eyes as if he had put aside all his shame and opened his mouth with difficulty.

"C-could we do it again?"

Whaaat?! You daring young man!

My insides tickled, my throat tickled, and my entire body tickled enough to make me squirm for a moment, but then I decided to accept his request and laid my lips on his once more.

It tasted like coffee.

Everything was so hectic.

I slept all day yesterday and woke up to Lily dragging me to the bathroom to scrub me clean in preparation for the wedding.

I rubbed my eyes and yawned repeatedly as I stood in front of the mirror, and Violet dressed me up and nagged at me to open my eyes properly so that she could put my make-up on.

When I retorted that Glen Hoffen-Roxburg and our officiant, the duke, would be the only ones to see my face, so it didn't matter if my makeup was crooked, my maidservants scolded me and asked me if I really wanted to walk around with wonky eyes for the only wedding of my life.

When I smarmily replied that it might not be my only wedding, Jack, who had come to work and was standing by my side, nagged me, too.

He snapped at me as he took Glen's side, asking me who on earth would marry me if it wasn't for Glen, and it made me wonder if he was my guard or Glen's.

Once I was prepared to leave the room, I told him to go be Glen's guard and linked arms with Aster. There was a lot of time left until the ceremony, and we were scheduled to parade in a flowered carriage in the morning.

I clambered into the roofless carriage with Aster, and we paraded around the entire duchy as I announced my wedding through a megaphone.

Our well-prepared citizens came out to congratulate me. They placed gifts in the carriage, threw flowers, let off fireworks, and went absolutely wild. I wondered if people got married just for this. *This is so exciting and nice.*

"Oh, all right then! Free drinks today everywhere in the duchy of Roxburg!"

Cheers and whistles exploded around me when I announced that I would pay for all drinks with my own money. I saw owners rush out of their stores, and one lady was holding her baby as she looked out from an open window on the third floor. *Checking the receipts that the bars and saloons would later bring to me would be a bigger issue than breaking my bank, but who cares! It's my one and only wedding!*

Now that I think about it, this is the first time I've succeeded in getting married in all my lives. It's such a happy occasion!

"Everyone who thinks I'm the most awesome person in the world, shout 'Rosalite Roxburg' three times!"

"You're the most awesome person, Lady Rosalite!"

"Oh my! You're so pretty, Lady Rosalite!"

No, I said shout my name three times.

Meh, I guess it's fine since everyone's excited. Drinks are free all day, and every single store is having a sale. Enjoy yourselves, and just don't make too much trouble. I'll have piles of work if you do.

As my eyes traveled down the guest list that I remembered to check on our way back, I saw that the royal representative, Four-breadth Princess, wouldn't be able to come because she was sick from drinking. I clicked my tongue at the news.

The fourth Imperial Prince of the Largole Empire also said he couldn't attend because it hadn't been a year since his mother's passing, and he's refraining from attending events even in his own homeland. *Everyone who's considered a bigshot isn't attending, then.*

That's not a good look for my wedding, but I guess I'll have to be satisfied with guests from the other duchies. Of course, Uncle Louis and his family won't be able to step foot on Roxburg land, but it's better that they don't come. Let them rot in the damn marquisate.

I greeted people as the carriage, embellished with flowers, continued onward to the wedding venue. The concertmaster was already playing music with his orchestra, and people were dancing out on the outdoor dance floor. They were already serving drinks and simple dishes, so I couldn't tell if this was a wedding or a social party, but I was told that this was how weddings went when people got married in our family, so I simply let them be.

After getting off the carriage, I met up with Glen. We greeted every relative, even those as distant as my third cousin twice removed or something.

It's strange that I haven't run into Asterion yet, but he's probably surrounded by men and women alike while he's being barraged with questions about when he's getting married. He grew up quite handsome, so I was sure he would be popular.

He'll probably never get married because of his obsession with his sister, though. Shitbag #1, #2, and #3 aren't here today, so maybe I can just relax and let him be pestered by other people.

Glen appeared exhausted after the rounds of greetings, but I couldn't let him rest. *We still have to do the wedding ceremony, the reception, and take care of the leftover work, so I can't let the groom rest.*

I patted his shoulder, changed into my actual wedding dress, and continued with the grand event.

The servants scattered to usher the guests to their respective tables, and the wedding march began as a course meal was served.

Since the duke was our officiant and I was concerned that entering separately wouldn't be a good look, Glen and I decided to walk down the aisle at the same time, hand in hand. We made our vows and listened carefully to the advice the duke gave us.

"I won't tell you not to fight, so just don't hurt each other when you do."

"Apologize immediately if you do something wrong."

"Bride, don't stick your nose where it doesn't belong and do try to keep your mouth shut."

"Groom, don't think too hard, and do learn how to express yourself with words."

"Live happily for a long, long time."

As we nodded and listened carefully to the words of advice that were valuable life lessons, I heard someone bawling from the nearest table.

Sir Sage was leaking tears and snot as he howled about how letting me go was such a sad waste. I decided to ignore him, and the duke scowled.

"Bride and groom, exchange your rings."

Duke, I know smoothing out your expression is difficult, but at least control your tone of voice.

Titters of laughter rang out from the guests because the duke was so blatant about his displeasure. Most of the laughter came from relatives. *They're probably fascinated because they've never seen him this angry before.*

Once the laughter had died down, my maidservants, dressed in bridesmaid dresses, brought the ring box. *Ah, I was wondering where they disappeared after dressing me up in my wedding dress. They went to change, too. I didn't realize it, but Violet and Lily are looking good, and the dresses look great on them.*

Hmm, I wonder if they have plans to get married. I know I could pay a lot for their dowry.

"Lady Rosalite."

Oops! How discourteous of me when my future husband is standing in front of me?

I held out a hand when I heard Glen call my name. He took out my wedding ring from the box and slipped it onto my finger with a solemn expression, and all that was left was for me to put a ring on his.

"?"

To my surprise, Glen quickly snatched his ring out of the box and slipped it on his own finger.

Sir? There are procedures, you know? It's my turn to put a ring on your finger. Hello? Mr. Future Husband?

"Let's get back to work if we're done here."

My mouth fell open in shock at Glen's confident statement. *We're done with our vows, yes, but we still have the reception. Why the hell would we go back to work?*

"...!"

At my confused stare, Glen, who had been so poised until a moment ago, blushed fiercely.

And because of that, I suddenly understood. I remembered.

Ah, I see, it's that.

Wow...! You were seriously upset about that all this time?!

"You really sulk for the longest time."

"I apologize."

"I should watch what I say forever if I don't want you to hold a grudge."

"I am sorry..."

What's there to be sorry about? I shouldn't have put the engagement ring on by myself back then.

Laughing to myself because no one else knew about the situation, Glen and I held hands as we walked back up the aisle amidst congratulations.

The wedding ceremony ended well, and no one objected to my marriage. I resolved to keep my guard up until the very end as I changed into my reception dress and went out to mingle with our guests.

This wedding was a joyous occasion, and even my future bankruptcy was a joyous occasion as well. I greeted everyone who had been pushed to the back of the list, including Luke Shatel, and made up my mind to enjoy the reception and this moment.

Once this dance festival is over, I'll have to go back to work. Consider me dead for the next week.

I didn't even get to go on a honeymoon, so I'll wear this to at least feel like I got married.

I grilled Violet until she helped me into my wedding dress and allowed me to wear it to the office. My guard of the day, Aster, was super excited to see me dolled up, and she said she had been too busy with security details to tell me on my wedding day, but I was the prettiest lady in the world. Then she gave me an adorable smile.

I thought Aster was only interested in food, but it turns out she has a real eye for beauty.

Strangely enough, Jack, John, the Crown Prince, and Four-breadth Princess always vehemently disagreed whenever I said I was beautiful, so I was infinitely grateful to Aster for being honest. *I'll give her half of my allotted snacks for the day.*

I had left for the office very early in the morning, so both Rion and Glen had yet to come into work. Instead, the commissioner of the public safety agency was hoping for an audience. Apparently having been waiting outside my office for a while, the old man who had been squatting down took off his hat as he stood up and bowed.

"I apologize for intruding so early in the morning, Lady Rosalite. I did send someone to congratulate you at your wedding, but I am deeply regretful that I could not attend myself."

"It's all right, Commissioner. Everyone and their mother know you're busy."

I can't even blame him for not coming because he probably had his hands full delegating traffic and people with my parade and gifting free booze. He's busy working instead of going to play his beloved golf, so what better news is there?

"Please, come inside. What brings you all the way here?"

As I opened the door and asked that he enter my office, the old man shuffled inside carefully and bowed once more.

No, don't do that. Why are you making me uncomfortable?

"I would like to apologize beforehand for relaying news that is sure to distress you. However, the matter being what it is…"

"What's going on?"

I asked him to have a seat and took mine at the head of the table. He let out a sigh and carefully spoke up.

"Several young people have been murdered recently. Most of them are either strong, adult men or well-known martial artists, and one of my own men has been killed as well."

"My, this is terrible news."

"But according to an eyewitness statement, the murderer's description…"

Wait, old man, why are you looking at me like that?

I urged him to continue, and the commissioner took another deep breath before uttering the name of his suspect.

"I am afraid… I must summon your guard, Jack Brown, to come in for questioning."

Jack Brown? The Jack Brown that I know?

CHAPTER
EIGHTY-ONE

"How exactly did the witness describe the culprit...?"

"Over 180 cm tall and dressed in black. It was too dark to see his face, but he was a skilled man with many different kinds of weapons."

Oh wow, yeah, that sounds like Jack.

But it's not like they nabbed him red-handed, so I can't just hand him over. I mean, I've got our duchy to think about.

"Jack wouldn't do something like that."

"Yes, I also did not expect you to hand over the criminal easily because he is from your family."

"I'm telling you; he isn't the one."

"I was merely hoping you would chastise him a little..."

"Jack would never kill civilians!"

When I slammed my palm on the table and yelled, the old geezer replied with a half-assed "All right," as though he was just letting me win. But then, he once again requested that I speak to my man—clearly unwilling to truly yield—before he left.

This dotard is still treating Jack like a criminal.

"Aster, bring Jack here at once."

"Are you going to hand him over to the public safety agency?"

"No!"

Child, why are you so hellbent on sending him away, too?

Then again, you two are always trying to end each other...

"Oh, and tell him to come to the printing room alone since this isn't something others should hear."

"Yup."

Aster saluted briskly and left to capture Jack.

I said what I said, but what do I do? Honestly, I couldn't think of anyone other than Jack who matched the description. A tall person in black clothing who knew how to use a variety of weapons and was skilled enough to kill someone from the public safety agency in one blow. *That indeed sounds like Jack.*

"..."

Come to think of it, Jack has been leaving the house during hours when people don't normally go outside to take Peter for walks...

No, no. Bad thoughts, bad thoughts! Don't think bad thoughts, Rosalite!

I crossed the doorway into the printing room and began pacing back and forth anxiously. *I do believe that it isn't Jack, but what if it is? If Jack's the one, then he has to have a reason, right? Maybe he's been stressed out since I haven't been giving him any take-the-life-of-another-human jobs, or...*

But still, he isn't one to just kill innocent people. What if the victim was a criminal? Yeah, that makes sense. He delivered punishment that a government institution failed to do. Yes, that has to be it. That's the only possible reason.

"I caught the culprit, little miss!"

I told you, he's not the culprit.

Just as I came to my own conclusions, the door of the printing room burst open, and Aster stomped inside confidently, dragging Jack by his hair.

Jack immediately stopped his stream of curses at Aster when he saw me, and then changed his words to something tamer to reprimand her.

"Let go, you crazy bitch!"

"Shut up, you goddamn psychopath killer!"

"Why am I a psychopath killer, pigface?!"

"Why are you giving me a compliment all of a sudden?! You're making me shy!"

I've already told you many times before, Aster, that that isn't a compliment. And I told you to make sure Jack comes alone, so why are you even in here?

"Good work, Aster. Now, take your leave so I can talk to Jack."

"…I'm sorry, what was that?"

"Get out."

When I waved my hand to shoo her away, Aster looked crestfallen and saluted once more before leaving the printing room. I wasn't sure what she was so upset about, but she kicked Jack in the shins before she left, which caused Jack to lunge at her like he was about to kill her. It took me a while to stop him.

"*Huff…Huff…*Why…*Huff…*can't you guys…*Huff…*just get along?"

"Thus is the fate of siblings, little miss."

"Rion and I get along fine."

"Maybe you're not siblings, then."

"Tsk, tsk!"

A half-brother is still a brother. Don't talk like that.

I stood on tiptoe and rapped his head with my knuckles before I told him my business. I glanced around and checked that we were the only ones in the printing room, as it wasn't time for Lem to come to work yet.

"Well, Jack, I uh... I wanted to tell you, uhm..."

"I'm listening, little miss."

"You take Peter on walks late at night, correct?"

"Yes, I do. People will get scared if I take him out in the middle of the day."

That's right, you're a good-natured boy who tries not to scare others. I nodded, proud of his big heart, and got straight to the point. *Jack is a good boy, so he'll probably tell me the truth.*

"The thing is, right when you take Peter for a walk... I mean, the timing is just perfectly aligned with when you take Peter out for a walk, you know? Every night, people are dying."

"Come again?"

"And the culprit, well, he's described as tall with black clothing and skilled enough to use many different weapons... So, I was wondering—"

"Are you suspecting me, little miss?"

Tsk, tsk! Like I said, it's not just that, okay?

I gave him some lame excuses and then took a deep breath before continuing. *It's partially my fault you're stressed, so this is the most I can do for you.*

"Listen carefully, Jack. We Roxburgs are on your side, no matter what. Just tell me the truth, and I swear on my honor I will protect you."

"That means you really are suspecting me!"

"No, I'm not suspicious. I'm saying, whatever the truth may be, I am completely and utterly on your side."

"Do I look like someone who'd kill random innocent people?!"

"Of course not! You don't! I've spent years with you!"

Why is he twisting my words? What I mean is that you are and will always be my guard, regardless of whether you've killed people or not!

I firmly told him my opinion, but it seemed like Jack took only the negative connotations to heart.

He stared at me resentfully for a moment before looking like he was about to cry, and then quickly slammed the gas mask he had clipped to his waist over his head and yelled.

"Stupid little miss! Idiot! Carnivore woman who only wants meat!"

What?! Of course, people need to eat meat!

Totally upset, Jack began storming away as if he was going to run away again. Recalling the days when he had gone missing, I hastily expressed my concerns to the back of his head.

"Jack Brown! I clearly told you that you may never run away again!"

"I'll be back to sleep!"

Then what about dinner, child?!

Ignoring my shout, Jack whipped out of the room. *I need to inform Madam Brown and the servants of the Brown residence if he's going to eat out, though.*

Well... it's Jack, so he'll figure it out just fine.

Thinking it wasn't such a big deal, I went back to work. That day, Glen got a nosebleed because we received all of the receipts for the drinks I had bought for everyone in the duchy. *I think I need to feed him soft-shelled turtle soup.*

I was in big trouble. Jack didn't come in to work for five days. According to Madam Brown, he returned to his room during the night to get some sleep, but then left when he woke up and didn't stay at the house at all.

During his absence, more people kept dying, and the commissioner asked to see me again. He broke a sweat as he demanded to know if I had chastised Jack, and I sweated hard as well.

The child didn't even stay home, but the number of victims kept increasing, and if he got caught in the act, I wouldn't be able to settle the matter myself, which meant that I would have to ask the duke for help.

After firmly denying that Jack was the culprit and sending the commissioner away, I popped a piece of bread into my mouth as my meal and went out to the promenade.

I haven't seen Jack since that day, and my darling Lord Glen has been avoiding me since he witnessed the soft-shelled turtle soup. Nothing is going right.

"Ughhh..."

As I plodded on, nibbling on my bread, and thinking about how everything in the world was meaningless, I heard the pattering of dashing feet.

It came from the rabbit hutch. Peter opened the door to his cuboid resting area by himself even though no one had pressed the bell, quickly came out to his yard, and bounced over the fence to land right in front of me. He then began stomping on the ground with his hindfeet.

You're raising dust, bunny.

"What? Are you claiming Jack's innocence, too?"

"Pwee! Pweee! Pwek! Pweek! Pweeek! Kyeee! Shyaaak!"

"Hahaha. I don't know rabbit language, you foolish brute."

"Pweeek!"

Huh, I guess he understands me, seeing how he's stomping even harder than before. Where the hell did Jack find this weirdo rabbit?

Fascinated by how smart he was, I reached out a hand to pet him. Peter smacked my hand away with his front paw. At the same time, Aster whipped out her sword in the blink of an eye, so I prioritized giving orders before checking my hand.

"Enough, Aster. I told you not to kill Jack's pets."

"But, little miss, it hit you first!"

"Enough, I say."

I just got a bit of dirt on my hand that's all. I took out a handkerchief from my coat pocket, wiped my hand, and then handed the dirtied handkerchief to Aster.

She glared at Peter after she stuffed it into her own pocket. Her sword was still out, expressing the fact that she still wanted to threaten him.

"Put the sword away. You're scaring him."

"It wouldn't be baring its fangs like that if it was scared."

"Peter, you too. Hide your teeth."

I scolded him gently, and Peter covered his fangs even as he stomped on the ground with his hindfeet. *He's a goddamn rabbit, so why are his fangs so big? Well, I guess it's weird that he eats meat in the first place.*

"Don't worry. I'm going to see what Jack's up to tonight."

I don't have to work late, so I'll have time to leave the estate. The excursion would take away my sleep time, but it was a small price to pay if I could only find out how Jack was doing.

"Do some laps around the track here even if Jack doesn't take you out for walks. You've gained weight."

"Pweee?!"

The duke had been feeding him so many snacks that Peter was getting chubby. Apparently understanding my comment, he let out a scream of shock and began hopping around the yard.

A fascinating beast indeed.

"Will you be leaving the estate tonight, little miss?"

"Yes."

"I will accompany you."

"Uh…"

I needed a guard, but taking Aster was dangerous. *If we run into Jack while he's in the middle of… of… uh… doing his thing, she'll excitedly drag him to the agency. I can't just let enemies meet at the worst time and in the worst place.*

"No, I'll take Carl or Quill this time. You should rest, too, you know."

"I cannot leave your protection in their hands. They might lose you due to being sidetracked in their excitement about getting to leave the estate."

Hearing you say the right thing sometimes makes me feel weird.

CHAPTER
EIGHTY-TWO

I gazed at Miss Aster Brown, who had a solemn look on her face, and tried to find a solution. *Will is rarely at home, and Sir Sage will probably destroy the entire duchy if I take him outside, but I can't ask Sir William because, you know... Sir William is the duke's guy.*

"I would feel at ease if you took Young Master Rion."

"Huh? Asterion?"

"Yes. The young master would probably beat Jack if it came down to pure skill. Though things might be different if Jack uses his tricks."

Is Rion that grown-up already? Wow, no way. He was only this big like a couple of days ago!

I couldn't accept Aster's explanation because the image of tiny Rion kept popping into my head. *I know Aster has no regard for Jack, but she's exaggerating too much.*

"I appreciate your high appraisal of Asterion."

"I didn't do that, though."

Just pretend you did.

Anyway... Asterion, huh...? Yes, he'd be more motivated to protect me, at least compared to Carl and Quill. He's got his sister-obsession fueling him, after all.

After reaching a compromise with Aster, I completed my inmate promenade and returned to my office. Then I quietly told Asterion about my plan. When I told him to join me tonight after dinner to take care of some business, just the two of us, he accepted my offer, saying he would follow me even if it killed him.

It is now night. The mafia... I mean, the stalkers should now confirm who the other stalkers are.

Having decided to meet up in front of the stables after changing into comfortable clothes, I saw Asterion running over, fully armed, and called for Elizabeth. We might lose Jack's trail if we waited any longer. We had to hurry.

"You're late. Hurry up and bring your horse."

"I'm sorry?"

Why is he staring at me like that? The beautiful Asterion, who was almost twenty, tilted his head, and I tilted mine along with him. The man who was staring at me straightened his head and spoke up as he scratched his cheek in embarrassment.

"Well... I do not have my own horse... sister."

"What?"

Wait, wait, wait. Neither the duke nor I bought you a horse all this time?!

Astounded, I asked him what horse he used to practice. The beautiful Asterion, who was almost twenty, replied that he simply took whichever horse was available and that he hadn't felt the need to buy his own horse because he never really left the estate.

E-even so... how can you not have a horse when you're almost twenty? What if you have to suddenly leave the estate?

"I-I see. I'm sorry, I didn't even notice."

"It is all right. I never really thought about getting a horse, anyway."

"Then, for now, the duke's horse is docile, so borrow—"

"Are we not going after Jack Brown? Then we do not need speed, so perhaps we can ride Elizabeth together?"

"Hm? Elizabeth?"

"Yes. We need to be stealthy, and two horses clip-clopping along would be too noisy."

"That's a good point."

Permitting his suggestion because it was logical, I secured Elizabeth's bit and ordered her to sit down.

But for some reason, she wouldn't listen.

"Sit! Elizabeth, sit!"

Pbbrrr.

What's wrong with her today? I stroked her neck cajolingly, but she just kept backing away.

She took a seat after clopping back about six paces, so I quickly hopped onto her back and motioned for Asterion to get on, but the damn horse sprang back onto her feet.

"Come on, Elizabeth. Be a good girl!"

Prrr.

Seriously, what's wrong with her? I thought it was strange, but now was not the time to cut her some slack.

I grabbed the reins to force her to stop and held out a hand to Asterion. Suddenly, Elizabeth began grunting and blowing as she shook her head fiercely, utterly displeased.

"Elizabeth, don't tell me…"

Pbbbrrr.

"Is Asterion not your type?"

Neigh!

I knew it. She had no problems letting Glen or the Crown Prince on her back, but she didn't want Asterion on her back.

"Miss Elizabeth, please, just this once. He says he doesn't have a horse to ride."

Pbbrr. Pbbrrr.

"What was that? Are you threatening him? We'll take Glen for a ride next time, so could you just bear with it this time? Just this once?"

Pbbrrr.

"Then how about a trip to the royal palace? I'll take you to the palace when I go, and we can go see the Crown Prince together."

Pbpphhh...

I see, the Crown Prince is more your type than Glen. You'll get in trouble if you just pick guys based on looks.

After I ran my fingers through her mane and calmed her with the promise of taking her to the royal palace, I held out a hand to Asterion.

Asterion grabbed my hand, put some pressure on it, and then jumped in place and onto Elizabeth's back.

The hell was that? I've only seen that in martial arts movies. Walking on air? Did you just walk on air? Like climbing air steps?

"I am ready, sister."

"All right, then."

I couldn't help but laugh at Asterion because he had gotten on Elizabeth's back in such a cool way but was now sitting super close to me with his face buried in my hair. *Elizabeth won't buck you off, even if you don't cling to me like that.*

"Now, Elizabeth, let's ride swiftly and quietly. We're trailing someone."

Pbbrrr?

She whirled her head around to look at me. *And now she's blinking like I'm out of my mind. Why does she keep trying to find something to complain about instead of just doing what I tell her?*

"Let's go."

At my words, Elizabeth moved her legs hesitantly, as if she were debating with herself on how to use them. Then she began running stealthily. Her hooves still made clip-clop noises, but they were quieter than usual.

She can do everything I ask. So talented!

As we cautiously neared the Brown residence, I saw Jack come out with his Death Scythe, which he rarely used, fully armed to the teeth. He leapt over the estate wall nearby.

What kind of acrobatic shit is that? The estate walls were three times the height of the average person, so I didn't think he'd be able to jump over them. Jack used his Death Scythe like a high-jump pole to get him off the ground, spun it over his head and embedded the blade end into the top of the wall, and then used his muscle strength to flip himself onto it before disappearing to the other side of the wall.

I saw what happened with my own eyes, but I still don't understand. Does everyone do shit like this when I'm not looking? Why is everyone acting like they're in a martial arts movie?

"Sister, let us go around."

"What? Oh, yes. Let's do that."

Rion's words brought me back to my senses, and I hurriedly steered Elizabeth to the front gates. Carl or Quill—I couldn't tell which—howled and hollered about where I was going in the middle of the night, but I coldly shook him off and followed after Jack.

I'm sorry, Carl, or maybe Quill. I'm busy right now.

I first followed the path next to the wall behind the Brown residence, but then it split into two. Just as I was deliberating on which road to take, I heard Asterion's voice from behind.

"Let us take the small path. I doubt he will take the bigger road with his large weapon in plain sight."

Yeah, the younger ones are always smarter.

I accepted his suggestion and turned Elizabeth onto the smaller path. However, we couldn't find Jack no matter how long we rode. *Did we miss him?*

"By the way, why are we following Jack?"

Oh right, I didn't explain anything. But I couldn't tell him the truth, either. *I mean, honorably, that is to say, in terms of the honor of both Jack and our duchy...*

"You don't need to know."

"I do not?"

"Yes."

Accepting my answer far easier than I had expected, Asterion voiced an irresponsible opinion about how we would run into Jack eventually and hugged my waist tightly. *Is he just out for the sake of being out?*

"Can't you at least try to look for him?"

"I can do that if it is simply trying."

"Yes. At least pretend to try."

So, stop rubbing your face in my hair. Doesn't it tickle him?

With Asterion hanging off my back like a piece of gum, I studied my surroundings. As telepathically connected with me as always, Elizabeth copied my head movements as she looked around as well and then suddenly pricked her ears.

She let out a whinny as if to warn me and slightly jumped in place to make me hold tightly onto the reins before she began galloping.

"What is it? Have you found Jack?"

Whinny!

Oh, she really wants to hurry up and finish the job so she can get Asterion off her back.

I told Asterion to hold on and let Elizabeth run whichever way she wanted. She left the small path and headed toward the brightly lit, wider road, eventually taking us to Blue Diamond Jewelry Avenue, which was the third most expensive bit of land in our duchy.

The sounds of steel clashing against steel were already ringing through the street. Not long after, a man wearing a black coat swung a scythe and slashed a man wearing a public safety agency uniform in half.

Blood spurted from him like a fountain, and the two halves of the dead man, who didn't even get to land a proper blow, rolled around on the ground.

I didn't spend money to get you an education just for you to slice innocent people in the middle of the street!

Infuriated, I jumped off Elizabeth and shouted at the man in the black coat.

"Jack Brown! I did not raise you like that!"

At my enraged voice, the man charged at me, his eyes flashing. He flicked the blood from his scythe and whirled it down to strike me, and I clenched my teeth as I thought about how Jack couldn't even recognize his master anymore.

I guess I'm dying a ridiculous death in this life.

While that thought ran through my mind, I realized the man's attack missed me. I hadn't dodged it, and no one had made me dodge it. It appeared as though the man had no intention of attacking me in the first place.

More than that, this man's face is different from Jack's. Jack isn't as handsome! And he's blonde! His hair is super shiny, too!

"Sister, move away from him!"

The man wasn't charging at me, but at Asterion. Asterion drew his blade immediately as the man swung his scythe, blocking it, and then twisted his sword to deflect it and close in.

Thinking that the man would be defenseless after that attack was a mistake. He pulled out a dagger out of nowhere and slashed it threateningly to create some distance between them.

He gripped the scythe that had been impaled into the ground with both his hands and yelled at Asterion, not even caring that I was behind him.

"I have no interest in the weak! Worry about yourself!"

Why was I feeling a sense of déjà vu right now? *I feel like I've seen this guy somewhere.*

EIGHTY-THREE

That attitude of his certainly reminded me of someone. *He uses a wide variety of weapons, is super strong, has shiny, blonde hair, and I can never have a proper conversation with him because it's like talking to a wall, and... and... I'm pretty sure he picked fights with random people for a really weird reason...*

"I shall give you my precious baby if you can defeat me!"

"...!"

Oh! I remember! Shitbag #2!

"Samuel of Zero Communication Skills!"

It was a long, long time ago. I only met him once in Life #3, but I gave him the title of Shitbag #2. Back then, when it hadn't been long since I first started being Rosalite Roxburg, I had gone for a walk outside, holding hands with Rion. We ran into that guy, and he just started picking a fight with us.

Samuel of Zero Communication Skills was a blacksmith. He had talent, but he tested his weapons by slicing people open. He was also famous for searching out people he deemed worthy of passing down his weapons to and vanishing afterward.

It's said that he's an elusive being who is hard to even meet in one lifetime, so why are Rion and I seeing him for the second time? What unfortunate destinies we have.

In Life #3, Samuel had crossed blades with Rion and felt that it would be worthwhile to groom him, so he... uh... said some weird stuff about the best flowers, blah blah, easy to pick, or whatever... and then he placed his mouth on...

I'll just stop there.

"You know who I am?"

The man, suspicious that I knew his name, turned around to address me, but I offered no response.

It's no use talking to him. He's got zero communication skills, after all. There's a reason I gave him that nickname. I had tried to talk to him many times back then, but he was practically a walking wall, so I had given up on communicating with him.

"Rion! Kill him! Bad things will happen if you don't!"

"Well, it does not matter either way."

That's right! Don't concern yourself with me! Just die!

Just wait, you prick. I'll blow you up myself, even if Rion doesn't manage to kill you.

Perhaps I had trained in magic just for this day. I had spent countless days crying and wallowing in bitterness after I lost Rion so meaninglessly that day. *You're the very symbol of the trial and error of my past. Die, asshole, die. Just die while you're at it!*

I readied my mana to skewer him with a bolt of lightning, should Rion fail to take him down. Once the conversion preparations were complete, I could spear him with my attacks using a simple activation spell. *Even if I mess up the coordinates, I can still limit his movements, but... damn it. I should have learned about guided attacks from Sir Sage since he lives on our estate!*

"A mage, huh?"

"...!"

Is his mana-sniffing skill on the same level as Aster? Apparently noticing that I was getting ready to use magic, Samuel tried to throw an assassination weapon at me even as he parried Asterion's attack.

At that moment, a pain shot through my shoulder. I felt the pain even though Samuel hadn't thrown his weapon yet, so I turned my head around and saw that Elizabeth was biting me. She clamped down on my shoulder and flung me to the side, apparently meaning to get hit with Samuel's weapon in my place.

"Elizabeth!"

I crashed hard into the ground and rolled a few times. My shoulder ached terribly, and I thought it might have been dislocated, but now wasn't the time to worry about my own body. *No! My horse! My only baby is going to get killed because of me!*

Clang!

I sprang to my feet, expecting Elizabeth to slump to the ground, but things unfolded differently from what I had expected.

Someone rushed to stand in front of Elizabeth. He swung his huge weapon, and six small daggers that Samuel had thrown scattered onto the ground. I saw a man crookedly wearing the gas mask that he normally wore fully over his face.

But even though he was the elusive Jack Brown, there was no way he could have "coincidentally" arrived at just the right time.

"Jack, you punk! You've been hiding and watching, haven't you?!"

"Yes, I have, and I can!"

What?! Why are you yelling at me when I, am the one who's supposed to be mad at you right now?!

I clutched my painful shoulder and blinked back tears as I was about to snap back at Jack. But then, on second thought, Jack hadn't made a move until now, and there was only one reason he would be angry.

"Uhm... Jack?"

"What?!"

"I was just wondering... Since when have you been watching us...?"

"Jack Brown! I did not raise you like that!"

"I'm sorry."

I didn't know what else to say, so I shut my mouth after saying sorry.

Yeah, he has every reason to be angry. Yes, yes, he does.

"I will gripe about that later, little miss!"

Thank you. Let's kill this guy first.

I had nothing to fear now that Jack was with us. Asterion and Jack had a rat's ass amount of attack coordination, but we were able to turn the tables on Samuel since we outnumbered him.

Asterion finally found an opening as Samuel was driven back by their attacks. He could kill the man in an instant if he just stabbed and sliced upward.

Feeling relieved, I was about to call Asterion's name, but he was acting strangely for some reason.

"...!"

"Tsk!"

His stab was shallow. Rion had hesitated at the last moment. Samuel was injured, but he had enough strength to escape. He discarded all of the weapons that would weigh him down and leapt into the darkness of an alleyway.

Did we just lose him?! I couldn't think of any words except those to scold Asterion.

"I told you to kill him!"

I did all of this so you could live! Idiot! Dumbass!

I smacked his back over and over again, my dislocated arm dangling. Pain seared through my shoulder from the force, but I was so pissed that I couldn't care less.

"That's enough, little miss! How would a novice kill someone?! This is probably his first actual fight, too!"

"Would *you* quibble about having experience if your life were on the line?! This little fool has grown up so sheltered that he can't even catch prey caught in a trap! Idiot!"

"Why don't we fix your popped-out arm first?! You'll damage the bone if you keep doing that!"

"Ahhhhh!"

Hoping to stop me from smacking Rion on the back, Jack grabbed my arm and shoved it back into its socket with a loud crack. Then he went over to Rion, who was apologizing profusely, and comforted him, telling him that the first time was the same for everyone.

Fine, I get it. No one is on my side. No one is on my side except for Elizabeth!

Feeling sorrowful, I rubbed my face on Elizabeth's muzzle. *Good girl, trying to get shanked instead of her master. My model horse, I'm going to give you a medal of honor and knight you when I get home.*

I have no choice but to go back to the estate and send people to find Samuel now. Thinking that I had to find Samuel of Zero Communication Skills no matter what, I grasped Elizabeth's reins to mount her. Suddenly, an ear-splitting crash resounded from the direction he had run off to.

It sounded like a building had collapsed. *What the hell happened?*

Finding it strange, I made Elizabeth gallop to the place where the sound had come from. When I arrived at the place where columns of dust were still rising from the ground, I saw the duchy residents poking their heads out the windows, woken up by the noise. I looked further and saw a bloody man crushed into a corner of the collapsed building.

The clothes looked like those of Samuel, but he had no body and was smeared onto the wall. That was the only way to describe it. Smeared. *Forget the fact that it's an amazing move. It's too gruesome.*

I climbed down from Elizabeth to investigate who on earth had done such an act, and then I shivered when I discovered three blades stuck into the ground.

What the hell? I'm cold. I can feel the chill. Instinctively, terror welled up inside of me. My body remembered.

No. I don't want to see it. But I have to. I'll die if I don't. I'll be killed.

Even as cold sweat poured down my back, I forced my feet toward the three knives with numbers on their handles. The stone floor was carved with elegant cursive writing, and it seemed that whoever did it used one of the knives to do it.

"Sharpen them."

"Hic. Hic! Hic."

Hiccups tore at my throat. *I want to cry. I can't breathe.*

Jack and Asterion, who had finally caught up to me, held me and asked if I was all right, but I couldn't handle the shock that I had already received.

"M-mother."

And with that one word that I barely managed to spit out, I lost consciousness.

From what I heard later from Jack, my eyes had rolled to the back of my head, and I frothed at the mouth, which was an apparently unsightly sight.

When I woke up, birds were chirping outside the window, and my shoulder was bandaged. I couldn't keep myself together last night because of the shock my heart went through, but I was a lot calmer this morning.

Aster, who sat next to my bed, repeatedly peeling peaches and shoving them whole into her mouth before sucking them dry like some leech and spitting out the pits, said that the duke had taken away the three knives that Jack had recovered as if they were precious to him. She also said that Jack and Asterion were scheduled to be on probation for three days as punishment for failing to protect me.

I was also at fault for only taking Rion without reserve, but it seemed the duke left me alone because he needed me to work. *Anyway, did Aster bring all those peaches only for herself?*

"Little miss. Have some."

"Thanks."

Finally. I get a slice.

I chewed on the peach and became absorbed in my thoughts. *Are moms supposed to be that scary?*

I didn't really know because I hadn't had a mom since I was very young, before I became Rosalite. After I turned into Rosalite, I never met her mom either, so I wasn't exactly sure what it meant by having a mom.

Neither the duke nor the people in the estate spoke much about her, and the only information I heard was "Rosalite Roxburg lived with her mother until she was ten" and "Her mother is YOLO-ing at her parents' house." *Come to think of it, Sir William bristles whenever he hears about my mother, saying that he'll kill her again. What the hell does he have against her?*

I had never visited my mother's parents' house where she was chilling, not in all my lives. *Which family is she from, anyway? It must be a pretty reputed family if she got married to a Roxburg. Only the duke's side showed up to my wedding, too. I didn't see a single hair from anyone on her side. I hadn't concerned myself with that because I left inviting relatives to the duke, but...*

"Huh...?"

Why is my mom so mysterious? And why did I shiver so much when I saw her handwriting? Well, that's because when I think of the word "mother," I...

"...can taste metal."

It feels like blood is pooling inside my mouth. I can also taste dirt for some reason. There's also a sour taste, like bile coming up from my stomach...

"Are you all right, little miss?"

"Yes... yes, I'm fine. I'm fine..."

I'm not going to think about it anymore. It's almost like I can feel the sensation of rolling in the mud as I get beaten spreading over my skin. I should just stop thinking.

Ugh. My body is trembling.

"Are you cold, little miss?"

Yeah. I think I am, kind of. Chills suddenly shuddered through my body like the day before, so I rolled myself up in a blanket that Aster brought over and accepted the peaches that she popped into my mouth. *I don't feel so great, but that doesn't mean I can take a break from work.*

I changed clothes with Aster's help and went to find the Roxburg physician with the blanket still wrapped around me. Thinking I probably had a cold, I had some medicine made and let the doctor check my shoulder again. Then I went to work as usual and received copious amounts of concern from Lord Glen.

CHAPTER
EIGHTY-FOUR

Apparently, the duke had taken care of matters after my eyes-rolling-to-the-back-of-the-head incident—because the commissioner came to see me not long after I went to work and apologized.

I thundered at him, telling him to stop bowing to me and instead apologize to Jack, whom he had wrongfully accused of being a criminal. I showed the old man where the Brown residence was because Jack was probably there, disciplining himself since he was on probation, and sent him away.

Jesus, look at all the shit I had to go through because that old geezer just had to come and talk to me about something ridiculous. Jack and Asterion are on probation because they couldn't protect me, and Jack hates me because I suspected him.

I contemplated how to make him feel better for a moment, and then decided to deal with things that I could handle first. So, I started to write up a certificate of appointment.

I called Violet over and revamped the mass-produced House of Roxburg Third-Rank Ribbon Merit. After ordering high-quality hay in bulk, I then knighted my beloved horse Elizabeth once all preparations were complete.

"I hereby appoint you, Elizabeth, as a knight of the House of Roxburg in honor of your bravery and loyalty to protect me without sparing yourself."

I gathered the people of the estate and held an appointment ceremony for Elizabeth, and then braided the ribbon into her mane.

My beloved horse would now sleep surrounded by the best hay in the land, eat the freshest vegetables from the stock brought in daily, and receive oil massages once a week.

After that, I dedicated myself to my work like an insane person in an effort to move past my PTSD associated with my mother. I switched out all the furniture in Asterion's room and introduced him to the horse breeder who had given me Elizabeth, so he could pick his own horse. I worked late every single day and even heard Glen tell me that there was no longer any work that I needed to personally look over.

That was a shock. *Yeah, it's only a day, but I can't believe I don't have any work.* The shock didn't end there.

Just as I was about to trudge back to my room because there was no work for me to do, I saw a royal carriage. Aster and I raced to the front doors with all our strength.

When we arrived, I was thankfully able to receive a banquet invitation from the Crown Prince. It had been a while since the last ball was held to find a wife for the Crown Prince, so Aster and I held hands as we danced.

However, the duke didn't appear, no matter how long we waited.

Wondering if he was sick, I visited his office, but he was perfectly healthy and working.

I waved the invitation around to tease him, but all he did was tell me to enjoy the ball.

It was terrifying.

The day before the ball, I got a facial and took the day off to rest. On the day of the ball, I got dolled up and headed to the stables with my servants in tow. I had a promise to keep today.

"Elizabeth! Are you there, my third-rank ribboned knight?"

Elizabeth trotted out proudly, her coat sleek and shiny. I brought the servants along because I had made a promise to her, but I couldn't help but feel anxious because she had never done anything like this before.

"Are you sure you can pull a carriage? If you want to see the Crown Prince, you'll have to drag that behind you with Aster and the horsemen riding in it as well."

I pointed to a carriage already hitched to a robust shire. I was planning on taking two carriages because I didn't like inconveniences, and pulling a carriage was hard work. Not only that, but Elizabeth also had to work in unison with the horse next to her.

I asked her if she could really do it since she had spent her entire life as a riding horse, and Elizabeth snorted derisively before trotting over to the carriage.

She looked back and forth at the servants as if to ask what the hell they were waiting for.

"Well... all right, then, if that's what you really want..."

Respecting Elizabeth's wishes, I climbed into the carriage. *I can't tell her no if she's willing to do all this to see the Crown Prince. I doubt she'll get another chance to ride all the way to the Crown Prince's palace like last time.*

Once preparations were complete, the carriages began rolling along a lot smoother than I had expected. That was one less thing to worry about, but another concern was still on my mind. I was worried about the duke.

The duke declining an opportunity to dance? Surely that's a sign of the end of the world. I wonder if something shocking happened to him, too. Otherwise, there's no way he wouldn't have been envious of the invitation I waved in his face. He's totally obsessed with parties and dancing! Hmm... what is this world coming to?

"Little miss."

Having been lost deep in thought, I only looked up when my escort, Aster, held my hand. I glanced out of the window. *Our estate really is close to the royal palace. We're here already?*

"Let's go, little miss."

"Wait."

Promising that I would bring the Crown Prince out to see her if I could, I left Elizabeth to the horsemen. I told them that I would send a message through a servant if I needed them, and then I walked toward the banquet hall with Aster.

I'm going to get in there, leave Aster where the food is, and then grab any man and bust some moves.

It would be so much better if Luke were here, but I shouldn't get my hopes up since he's such a busy boy. Maybe I'll summon John Brown if I can't find a partner, since he's probably just taking care of the hungover Four-breadth Princess in her palace. Or maybe I'll just dance the male part. If worst comes to worst... I guess I'll have to pull Aster from her food.

I feel bad for Aster, but I really need to dance. There had been too many psychologically draining incidents recently. *I'm going to play all day, spend the night at the Crown Prince Motel while his maidservants serve me, sleep as much as I want, and then go back home.*

Immediately after stepping into the ballroom, I took Aster to where the food was laid out. The other noble ladies who attended the Crown Prince's wife-searching party came up and greeted me, but I only had time to vaguely nod in response and pass by.

I need to get Aster to the food and hurry up and start dancing.

"Why did it take so long for you to get here?!"

Jesus Christ, what the hell, man?!

I jerked in surprise at the angry yell and looked around to find the owner of the voice. *You can't just shout like that when I'm on the brink of a nervous breakdown. My poor heart.*

"Come."

The person who approached me as he yelled was none other than the star of the find-a-wife ball, the Crown Prince. Theodore the Smiling Face was quite unlike himself, with a strange expression on his face that didn't look like a smile or anything similar. I stood there, staring blankly at him because of the sudden demand that I follow him.

Theodore marched ahead a few paces, apparently certain that I would follow, and then glanced behind him and saw that I wasn't there. He plastered a mean smile on his face and walked back toward me.

"I told you to come, did I not? Are your ears malfunctioning?"

"I am not in the mood to serve you today, Your Highness."

"Lady Roxburg, you always beckon the dignified Crown Prince to and from, and yet you will not do as he says? How irreverent."

"You should become a Roxburg if you are so chagrined."

"Your nonsense is as exceptional as ever."

"Someone who understands my nonsense must be nonsensical as well."

"Just come when you are told. Why are you talking so much?"

"You already know that I'm talkative, Your Highness. It saddens me that you have socialized with me for this long without that knowledge."

The moment I was done talking, the Crown Prince reached out to grab my hand, but I snatched it away.

He reached out in the direction I had removed my hand to grab it again, but I yanked it down once more.

Oh, he looks mad.

"I shall summon a royal guard."

"Did you say you would summon a royal guard to capture a delicate woman?"

"Yes."

He's really mad.

He'll probably collapse from rage if I keep this up, so I guess I'll just call it quits here. I held out my hand to Theodore and meekly let myself be captured and dragged to wherever he wanted to take me.

For whatever reason, he stomped across the dance hall where everyone was dancing, entered one of the lounge rooms that had been prepared for honored guests, and slammed the door shut.

After thoroughly examining the area to make sure no one was there, he stood before me and cleared his throat.

"Ahem. I brought you here because…"

The Crown Prince gazed at me from head to toe, and his eyebrow twitched. He took a step back and cautiously opened his mouth.

"…you seemed to have something you would like to confess to me. So, speak."

What?

I tilted my head in confusion, unable to decipher his intentions.

If I was a noob who didn't have much experience living as Rosalite Roxburg, I would've probably spilled whatever I felt guilty about. *After all, our duchy has spies in the royal palace and all over the Alain Kingdom, planted there by any and all means. We monitor all possible threats and their every move so we can protect the Crown's peaceful life.*

But the Rosalite I was now would never make a mistake like that. My plans were always perfect, and there was no concern about any information leaking.

I only use people who were proven to be able to keep a secret through my many lives, and I'm meticulously keeping the mouths of every spy who's done with their work shut forever. Dead men can't speak, after all.

That's why I'm totally confident right now! I have nothing to feel guilty about!

"What might you be speaking of, Your Highness?"

"I already know everything. You need not be embarrassed."

"Already know what, exactly?"

The Crown Prince coughed and cleared his throat for a while, making me wonder if he had contracted some kind of lung illness since he enjoyed hanging out with the second prince. *That sounds serious. I should call the doctor. The Crown Prince may have an awful temper, but he's still going to be someone who holds up the country. He can't have lung problems.*

"About the fact that you like me."

"I already told you that before, Your Highness."

"What...?!"

I had already told him that I didn't not like him back when I gave him the doll as I endured all kinds of shame surging up inside me. *Why is he talking about that again?*

"Do you not remember? I informed you that I didn't dislike you when I gave you the Rosalite Roxburg Mach II."

"Are you saying that garbage was a confession of your feelings?"

"Calling it garbage is a bit harsh."

Do you even know how embarrassing it was? Saying it like that was putting it nicely, and even that felt like centipedes and millipedes crawling over my skin. Calling it garbage... How dare this child belittle my sincerity?!

"I see... I suppose I went too far."

"It is all right if you know you did."

"But if that is the case..."

Now what?

I pressed him, wanting to hurry up and go dancing, and the Crown Prince questioned me with a confused look on his face. *I've never seen him like this in all my lives. I wonder if he's in critical condition because of his lung disease.*

"Why did you marry that man?"

"That man? Might you be speaking of Glen Hoffen Roxburg?"

"Yes, him. Glen."

"Because... he's a competent worker?"

"Are you saying that you decided to get married because he does his job well?"

"Yes, Your Highness."

Haha. This is interesting. The weirdest expression ever crossed the Crown Prince's face at my words, and that wasn't all. He paced in place in a figure-eight pattern like a honeybee for a moment before coming back to stand in front of me. Then he started yelling at me as if he were angry.

"You cannot resolve to marry for such a ridiculous reason! It is discourteous to your partner!"

He bellowed resolutely and eventually grabbed my shoulders and shook me back and forth. My eyes began spinning in my head, and I couldn't keep my balance. *I need this to stop. My brain is rattling around in my skull.*

"Who cares?! It's just a contract! The contract renews itself every two years, and I will let him go if he finds someone else he wants to marry!"

"How does getting married under a contract make sense?! And you call yourself a human being with a heart?!"

"Well, stuff like that happens sometimes!"

EIGHTY-FIVE

Unable to bear it any longer, I thrust the Crown Prince's hands off of me and clutched the wall. I felt like throwing up. *The entire world is spinning.*

"W-what kind of woman are you?!"

That's my line, not yours!

I was clearly the victim here, but the Crown Prince acted dramatically like he was the one who got hurt as he insulted me by calling me the most vicious of all wicked people and tried to leave the room.

I would have let him leave under normal circumstances, but I had a request. *I promised my precious horse Elizabeth many times that I would help her meet the Crown Prince, and I can't break that promise now.*

If the Crown Prince refused, I would probably invade his palace later, but that was something I could think about later.

"Wait. Please make some time for me later—if it is all right. There is someone who wishes to see you, Your Highness."

"Tell them to make an official request through the proper procedures."

"She cannot do that, for she is a beast."

"Well, I do not care."

"I know a contractor who does exceptional antibacterial waterproofing construction to prevent mold."

"What does that have to do with me?!"

The Crown Prince roared and slammed the door to the lounge room. His stomping footsteps grew fainter.

I knew he would come back, so I decided to give him just thirty seconds. *One, two, three, four, five...*

I counted slowly, and when I reached twenty-five, I heard footsteps outside again. Completely different from his proud demeanor earlier, Theodore meekly opened the door and stepped lightly to stand in front of me. His usual sweet, Crown Prince smile was on his face as he spoke to me in a tender voice.

"What you said... is it true?"

"What would I gain by telling you a lie, Your Highness? The contractor renovated my office as well."

"And the cost will be covered by the House of Roxburg?"

"The Bank of Roxburg shall provide you with loan consultations, provided you bring the required documents."

"Do not be so miserly when you have more than enough money."

"That money comes from my miserliness."

The Crown Prince glared at me and spread the fingers of his right hand, telling me of a condition in which he yielded considerably. *I know there's nothing for him to gain from being stubborn, but he's giving up so easily.*

"Half. We are both responsible for putting the second prince in that place, so why don't we pay for half each?"

"As it is you, Your Highness, I shall consider our relationship and give you a loan without interest."

"This is not appropriate between ruler and subject. In what world does royalty borrow funds from his vassal?"

"As a recent example, His Majesty the King borrowed the entirety of the construction costs for this royal palace from His Grace the Duke ten years ago."

"Yes, every generation of your family is so... wonderful."

"You give us too much praise, Your Highness."

To be honest, the king has yet to repay us, but I'm not going to tell the prince that. It'll set a bad example.

For me, just making the Crown Prince feel indebted to me makes it worth spending money. He's a good kid who thinks about his younger brother. The construction cost isn't even that expensive for me anyway.

"Then I shall take my leave, Your Highness. I pray you will get married this year."

"Do you not have anything else to talk to me about other than marriage?"

"Make a baby. It does not matter if it is a boy or a girl. Let us raise the child magnificently."

"The mother of the country at heart, I see."

"Not only the mother, Your Highness. I intend to live long and become the grandmother of the country as well."

And just to be clear, if you do have a baby, I'm not going to raise him like you. I'll raise him so he's kind and obedient, doesn't need naptimes, and doesn't wash his hands raw just because someone's lips touched them. I would raise him to be both mentally and physically healthy.

I told the Crown Prince a smidgen of the ambitions held in my heart, and his lips quivered as though he was looking something ghastly. He put some distance between us.

"Who said I'd make you the mother of this country? Absolutely ridiculous."

"I am just saying, Your Highness. Do you not know what a metaphor is?"

I recalled how hurt I had been when Jack said that to me before, so I used it against the Crown Prince. However, the Crown Prince really didn't seem to know what a metaphor was, and he only gave me a look of hatred before leaving the room.

I guess he didn't take any intensive courses in Alainian or literature because they rushed his crown prince education. I'll send him some literary classics along with the construction funds later.

There are so many amazing works of literature in the Alain Kingdom. This is why you shouldn't rush your education. Look at Four-breadth Princess. She's received a decent education since she was young, and that's why she isn't lacking in terms of refinement as well.

I wouldn't have had to grapple with Theodore and plague him to bring me a successor if the princess just didn't drink. *Those damn eyes. Damn those eyes of hers.*

"Oh dear, Your Highness. You cannot simply leave before we agree upon a time."

I hurriedly chased after the Crown Prince to schedule a meeting after the banquet. He played hard to get, saying that he didn't want to see a woman like me in private, but then gave in and said he would dance his last dance with me and meet the one who wanted to see him. I went to prepare for their encounter.

Aster was eating with all her might, and there was no one who seemed able enough to be my dance partner, so I asked Four-breadth Princess if I could borrow John, who was indeed servicing her hangover needs. We danced together for a while.

Maybe it's because he's been at the royal palace for a long time. He knows a lot of moves and dances well, too. The princess hadn't been present at any banquets these days, so the fact that his repertoire was stuck at about five years ago was a flaw, but it didn't matter because I liked old-school dancing, too.

Still, I really wish Luke were here. Is he too busy to attend today?

"How much longer do I have to dance, little miss?"

Tsk! I haven't had this much fun in a while, so why can't he just go along with it?

John seemed to be getting bored after dancing with me for a whole hour, and he made an excuse about being worried about Princess Grace and requested that he be excused. *She's passed out with a hangover. What is there to take care of? All you were doing was staring at her sleep when I went there earlier.*

"Until the end of the night."

"Make Aster do it."

"How could I make her do it? She's eating right now."

"So, am I to be exploited without even being fed?"

"You have great mileage. And your owner gave me permission."

"You caused a ruckus by screaming songs next to an ill person."

Well, she shouldn't have done something to make herself so ill, then. No one forced her to get drunk and bedridden.

When I pretended that I couldn't hear him and tittered, John grabbed my hand and twirled me around over and over again. It made me dizzy, but it was bearable.

"Do you think I'll let you go if you do this?"

"Do you know why Aster serves you so well, little miss?"

"What kind of trickery is this?"

Is he trying to pit us against each other because nothing he does will make me let him go? But Aster would never talk badly about me behind my back, and I trusted her, so John's tricks wouldn't work.

John, I'm going to dance with you, no matter what you tell me.

"We had beef short ribs at the Brown residence on the day you were born."

"..."

"I assume His Grace sent some to every employee in celebration of your birth. It was the first time Aster had ever eaten such a meal, and she later cried and even wrote a poem. Would you like to hear it?"

"...That's enough."

"Perhaps thou art called short ribs because of the short time it takes to eat thee."

"Stop!"

Please stop, it's too lame!

I decided to let John leave because I didn't want to hear any more. As I pushed away the man wearing his royal guard uniform on his chest, the little son of a dog gave a satisfied smile and bowed.

"I shall attend with Princess Grace the next time we meet, little miss. Goodbye."

Yeah, yeah. Fine, go. Go find your master.

Feeling drained after sending John away, I headed toward the edge of the ballroom. *I can't waste the Crown Prince's time since he needs to find a wife, Aster's still eating, and the other young lords all run away if I get close because they're scared I'll ask them to dance.*

If Duke Edanelli were here to goof off, I'd try to ask him to dance, but he isn't here either. Damn it.

I feel bad for Aster, but I guess I have no choice but to cut her eating time short. There was still quite some time left for the ball to end, so I felt like I was wasting time.

"Oh my, Lady Rosalite!"

A woman I didn't know called me as I stood there looking for Aster. Someone I didn't know calling my name wasn't something new, but I felt kind of bad because she was clearly from the House of Edanelli.

She had tan skin and red hair, with curves that were exactly like Lady Dorothy's. I was nothing but apologetic because she looked like she was a close relative of the main family, yet I couldn't remember who she was.

"Do you know who I am?"

"Might you perhaps have no one to dance with? Please wait a moment! I have been waiting for this day!"

Despite her mature image, the woman fussed and waved her arms about as she asked me not to move a muscle. *Haha, she's cute, but what is she trying to do? She's even making me wait.*

"Lady Rosalite!"

I waited for the woman as she requested, and she came dashing out of the hallway that led to the lounge rooms after having borrowed the clothes of a servant.

She had removed all of the accessories and embellishments that she had on and changed into more comfortable clothes and shoes. She giggled as she held out a hand to me.

"I am grateful, but changing your attire makes dressing up for this banquet quite meaningless..."

"It's all right, Lady Rosalite! Let's go!"

Without hesitation, the woman dragged me to the middle of the dance floor and took the lead. I was a bit anxious at first, but I soon realized that she danced the male part of the dance amazingly.

"How are you so great at dancing the man's moves? What a strange lady you are."

"I practiced, Lady Rosalite. I told you. I have been waiting for this day."

Exactly. You said you've been waiting for this day, so what reason do you have for practicing the male dance moves?

When I kept chattering away because I felt bad that she was spending her time with me when she was probably here as a wife candidate for the Crown Prince, and because I still couldn't remember her name, she wrapped her arm around my waist and pulled me close as she leaned her face in.

"Do not concern yourself, Lady Rosalite. I am requesting that you please give me your time."

Oh my, my, my! What is going on? Please don't do this! I'm a married woman. Heavens me!

I responded exaggeratedly and lightly smacked her a few times on her shoulder, and the woman beamed and continued to dance.

Anyway, a married woman, huh? Hehe. Married woman. Yeah, it's a contract marriage, but I'm still married. You live and you learn, eh?

We danced excitedly, changing styles whenever the music did. In what seemed like no time at all, we saw the Crown Prince approaching us, having rotated through all of his future wife candidates. *I should finish up here and go get Elizabeth.*

With that thought in mind, I thanked the lady of Edanelli, and she said it was her pleasure and pushed me toward the Crown Prince.

"The evening air is still chilly, my lady. Please enjoy the rest of the night."

Hm?

Feeling like I had heard that line before, I gazed at her with wide eyes. The woman smiled playfully and pretended to wrap something around her shoulders.

Huh? What? No way. Are you... you're not the... Are you her, child?!

"You gave me that shawl, so it's mine now. I shall not return it, Lady Rosalite."

Oh my God, that little baby grew up this big?!

CHAPTER
EIGHTY-SIX

The woman waved, said goodbye, and soon she was far away. However, seeing how much she had grown since the time she cried about not being able to dance with the Crown Prince just hit me differently.

Wow, I see... it's already been that long...

"..."

Wait, why is Theodore still not married when it's been that long?

Getting infuriated at the thought, I glared at the Crown Prince, and he cursed at me as he told me not to be so blatant with my nasty temper.

After hastily finishing the last dance with the Crown Prince, we went to the front garden of the Crown Prince's Palace, where Elizabeth was waiting. I had him mount her on his own before I slapped Elizabeth's hindquarters to encourage her to start.

I shouted at Elizabeth to not let him down until she ran three laps around the palace, and Elizabeth enthusiastically galloped away with the Crown Prince on her back for a nighttime stroll.

I thought I heard the Crown Prince hurling insults at me again, but I couldn't hear him anyway because he was too far away.

Feeling a bit better, I took the maidservants from his palace and headed to the guest chamber. I had visited the place so often that it felt like a second home to me.

"Ugh…"

I don't want to go home.

I glanced once at Aster, who was already sprawled in bed and snoring, and then lay my head on the table.

Usually, I didn't want to go home because I didn't want to work, but this time was different. I didn't want to go home because the duke was acting strange, Glen was making me walk on eggshells, and Asterion was acting distant.

The duke being weird wasn't too stressful since I could just stay in my own office. However, having to sit and work between Glen and Asterion in the same room was grueling.

Why is the atmosphere always so uncomfortable? They seem to have a fairly good relationship with each other. Or maybe they don't? Well, they wouldn't have agreed to work in the same room if that were the case. Is it all my fault, like Sir William says? I don't know what I did wrong, but is it my fault?

I was already uncomfortable working between them, but Lord Glen grouched at me whenever he could ever since I fed him soft-shelled turtle soup, and Asterion didn't even talk to me these days.

When we did talk, all we did was greet each other in the mornings and evenings, and we never had long conversations for some reason. *I think it's probably because I hounded him back when we went out that night, but I can't blame him for that because that really is my fault.*

Now that I think about it, Jack was right. How can a kid who's fighting in real life for the first time actually kill someone? Of course he would hesitate.

The hell. I brought everything except the duke thing on myself. I should have asked Lord Glen if he could eat soft-shelled turtle soup before feeding it to him, too.

But I mean, come on, doesn't everyone eat that? It's food. It's yummy, too.

Creaaak.

As I sat there, immersed in thought, the balcony door of the guest chamber opened, and a man swathed from head to toe in black slinked inside. He watched me as he uncovered his face in a leisurely manner, and...

"Agh!"

...I let out a belated scream.

"Aghhh!"

The man also screamed in surprise at my scream.

We screamed after looking at each other, and Aster suddenly sprang up from her snoring slumber and attacked the man. Or rather, she *tried* to attack the man.

Though she had already seen the man's face since he took off his mask, Aster swung her fist at him, pretending that it was a mistake. Not long after, her mouth had an intense make-out session with the marbled floor.

The man casually tripped Aster, who was much bigger than he was, and grabbed the back of her neck to throw her down effortlessly.

Aster cartwheeled onto the floor like a hamster wheel. *Fwip*. Just like that. *Fwip*.

Smashing face-first onto the marble, she thrashed around as she groaned in pain. The man barely spared her a glance and then lost interest as he walked toward me, rubbing at his chest.

"Why did you scream like that? You scared me, little miss."

"It's because you snuck into a guest chamber of the Crown Prince's palace in the middle of the night. It's not even our house!"

"That's why I made my presence known and came through the door."

"Yes, yes. The balcony door is still a door. It's my fault. It's *all* my fault, isn't it?"

Expecting a shred of common sense from Will Brown was indeed my mistake. After blaming myself a few times, I asked Sir William's third son if he would like a glass of water.

When I explained that I couldn't get him tea because the maidservants would be surprised if they saw a man who had no reservation to stay at the Crown Prince's palace, but I could get him some water, Will took a seat at the table and said he would gratefully drink a glass.

I guess what he has to say is going to take a while.

"Now, to what do I owe the pleasure of having the busy Will Brown visit me?"

"It appears that there will be a great change in personnel within the Shatel Corporation."

"Hmm..."

That is interesting information, but was it necessary for him to come tell me that when I'm hanging out at the palace?

When I crossed my legs, looking dissatisfied, Will quickly gulped down his glass of water and placed it back on the table before continuing.

"It appears Luke Shatel will return to his homeland."

"Is that right?"

"You are close with him, are you not, young mistress?"

"Well, I can't say that we are close or anything…"

"You summon him to the estate every month and sometimes every week to dance and spend time together without informing His Grace, and then secretively send him back home. What do you call that if not close?"

"Yes, Luke and I are close."

This kid already knows everything.

I decided to admit it after first trying to deny it. I warily asked if the duke knew, and Will said he hadn't told the duke because it was my private life.

Oh, thank God. The duke almost got to steal my dance buddy. I was sure that the duke would snatch Luke away from me if he found out because Luke was really good at dancing with men, too. Even Luke would hop on the duke train in a flash because buttering him up would be better for business.

Well… he's going back home, so he won't get to play with either me or the duke…

"I am informing you so that you do not make an enemy out of the Shatel family and deal with your affections on your own."

"Deal with what affections? Luke says he's returning to his homeland, so I simply need to send him off well. And we're just dance partners..."

"I pray it is as you say."

I offered some cookies to Will, but he said he didn't want any because he didn't want crumbs all over him and instead said he would accept something like hard candy. *Yeah, I bet he's low on sugar from running around everywhere.*

"I only have cinnamon-flavored ones. Is that all right?"

"I like cinnamon."

Okay, good.

I reached into the little pouch tied to my underskirt and pulled out a piece of cinnamon-flavored candy. After unwrapping it, I popped it into Will's mouth. *He's eating it so well. Aster always bites down and shatters the hard candy as she chews, so it's terrifying to watch, but Will eats quietly like a normal person.*

"I heard the duchess passed by the area recently, young mistress."

"What? Oh... yes, she did."

"Then that means that Young Master Asterion's birth mother is nearby as well, so please be careful."

"?"

Asterion's mom is alive? But what does that have to do with my mom?

I had never heard anything about that before and didn't understand what the two mothers had to do with each other, which meant that I had absolutely no idea why I needed to be careful. I pried and interrogated Will, and he stared blankly at me as if he were the one who didn't understand.

"His Grace did not tell you anything?"

"Nope!"

"Then I shall not as well."

No! Tell me! You can tell me! Hey! Tell me before you go!

I wanted to tie him up if I had to so I could make him talk to me, but Will jumped to his feet. Stomping on Aster, who was still on the floor, on his way, he slipped back out of the balcony door and left.

I thought Aster would at least try to grab one of his legs, but she had been out cold with her face smooshed into the floor. She sprang upright and whipped her head around.

...Aster, you have a double nosebleed.

"Will Brown! Where is that asshole? Will Brown!"

"He just left after stepping on you."

"Damn!"

Quiet. Let's get you cleaned up.

I got a handkerchief from my pocket and grabbed Aster's nose. Thinking it would be all right since Will was gone now, I shouted for anyone waiting outside, and two maidservants came inside to help.

The two girls were taught well and didn't ask what happened, but my guilty conscience made me make up some story about how Aster fell on her face while jumping on the bed. The maidservants wholeheartedly accepted my explanation without question.

I don't know about anywhere else, but that's Aster's reputation here at the Crown Prince's palace.

I'll have so much to do aside from work when I get back home tomorrow.

I need to console both Glen and Asterion, ask about why I need to be careful of Asterion's birth mother, and... ask about my own mother...

The truth is that I avoided any conversation about my childhood as best as I could because I knew nothing about my life before sixteen but fainting and frothing at the mouth because of an encounter with my mom was just weird.

If the duke is surprised, I'll just say I have memory loss and ask him about it. He's pretty flexible with what he accepts, so he'll probably think memory loss is a possibility. After all, he calmly said, "I suppose that could happen," when he thought I had forgotten every last bit of my successorship education. He just taught me again from scratch.

I decided to think about everything tomorrow and went right to sleep the moment Aster's nosebleed stopped.

Early the next morning, as my carriage was being prepared, I noticed an axe embedded in the middle of our family crest on the carriage. I grabbed the axe, struggled to pull it out, and then flung it through a window near the front entrance of the Crown Prince's palace. The window shattered with a loud crashing noise, and I heard the Crown Prince shouting something about locking me in the dungeons for crimes against royalty or whatever, but I pretended not to hear anything and went back home.

That's what you get for destroying other people's property. Not to mention that there's only one obvious reason he's awake at this hour when he usually sleeps in all the time.

To be continued...